The
REVOLUTIONIST

DeEarlon

Barking Cat Books

An Imprint of New River Press

Cover and interior design by New River Press
Contributing Editor: Laura Elaine

Published by Barking Cat Books
An Imprint of New River Press
645 Fairmount St., Woonsocket, RI 02895
(888) 273-1941

www.NewRiverPress.com

Library of Congress Cataloging in Publication Data applied for.

ISBN 978-1-891724-19-0

Printed in the United States of America

Dedication

To all those who have ever been in this situation,
and to those who might be.

To John Adams, second president
of the United States of America
and
Thomas Jefferson, third president
of the United States of America:
*Though you did not agree on everything,
on this you were both right.*

Contents

Introduction

Setting: The United States of America in the future.

They had come seeking freedom, and they found it. A century and a half later, it was suddenly and rudely torn from them, so they fought. Miraculously, they won.

For more than two centuries, with a squall in the middle, their freedom continued. Suddenly and rudely, their freedom was torn from them again, from the inside. But this time many had grown fat and passive. Little by little their freedom was sucked away as they were distracted by a myriad of shallow pleasures.

Now, about to lose all, something happened in America.

This book would not have been possible without the utter fiascos taking place in my nation as I write this.

It is a work of fiction. Any resemblance to actual people, places or situations is purely coincidental. For now. All character names are fictitious.

I recall the words of Thomas Jefferson. "The tree of liberty must be refreshed from time to time with the blood of patriots and tyrants."

And those of Winston Churchill. "Those who do not study history are condemned forever to repeat it!"

-DeEarlon

Chapter One - Del.

Life isn't fair, yet it goes on. The ants understand this better than we humans. Someone told me that once and, every so often, that thought flashes through my mind.

It's strange. Despite everything going on around me, all I can think of is Barb and the kids. Barbara, oh God! And the kids. God please keep them safe!

I look around me. All I see is dirt, smoke and bodies. Some are even alive.

What am I doing here? What are any of us doing here? I'm crouched, cold, wet, hungry and scared to death.

I look down the line in both directions. Everyone is huddled low, behind this dirt and grass berm, clutching their weapons, and everyone looks just like me. They're covered with mud, tired, and all have wide, glassy, bloodshot eyes. I laugh because I must also have those eyes.

That question: What am I doing here? It really has two answers. The first is a history of what got us into this situation in the first place; so many situations over the last few years in this country, every one of them leading us here. What does it really take for people to rebel against the government of the nation that gave them birth; to take up arms against that government and put their own lives in jeopardy?

Slowly, over the hours and days, my mind is pulling up and checking off those events.

The second answer, or question as it were, is more technical and even mundane. Why are we in a line in what amounts to a trench? Troops forming a line and fighting from a long trench is something no military force has done for a long time. It's a dangerous, archaic strategy in a modern world.

General Ordway, though, says we have to fight this way for now. The reason, he says, will become obvious soon. It had better become pretty damned obvious pretty damned soon because we're losing a lot of men this way.

It's quiet now. All you can hear is the wind blowing. Not like two hours ago. Then terror, hell, fire, and the low moan of the dying filled the air. One of those men was my friend, Tom Neil. He was so gung-ho in the beginning. If I turn my head, I can look back at him now, but why? Who's going to bury him? I laugh again. Hell, who's going to bury me?

I look down the line again. Paul's coming. He's the runner. Our communications went out over two days ago, but Paul goes up and down the line with messages and info now. Al Beaulieu used to do that, but he got shot. I check my ammo. Only 70 rounds left. Breathing hard and deep, I fall back against a giant tree stump that juts out of the berm. Paul will be here soon enough. I'll wait for him.

My head tilts back and I stare at the sky. It's what we used to call a beautiful day. A few white, puffy clouds drift through the azure heavens. Too bad we have to look out over a scorched, pock-marked, smoldering field. Nothing to do now but wait.

"Wait for what?" I ask myself. For Paul or for death? Probably both. I heard tanks moving up on the other side a few minutes ago. That will be it. That will be - it!

I search down deep. How did you get here, Jimmy Boy? How in hell did we all get here?

Fourteen years earlier

"Come here, you!"

"James Lamberti, you pervert. You're absolutely insatiable! My mother warned me about men like you. Now here I am married to one! Jim, stop! We have to go to lunch."

"Barb, we'll have the rest of our lives to go to lunch, but you only get one honeymoon!"

"But I'm hungry now! What if I faint from hunger in the

middle of...well, you know."

"No one ever fainted from hunger then."

"Oh really! And you know that how, Mr. Genius?"

Big sigh. "Alright, alright, we'll go to lunch. That should prove my undying love for you!"

"Oh, you're such a martyr! Then, after lunch, we'll go check out those cute little shops along the docks."

Another big sigh from me. "Oh! You have no idea how much of a martyr!"

Back then, no one thought anything about it. It was the way things were in this country. You grew up, and, after graduating from high school, either got a good job or went to college so you could get a better job. It was the rhythm of life back then, and it was a pretty good rhythm.

If you grew up in suburbia, like me, you did certain things and looked forward to certain passages in your future. I had a part-time job and I was living at home, as were many of my friends. College is the thing, everyone said. So I started going to night school. That's where I met Barbara, a tall, raven-haired beauty. Her father was well known in town and the owner of two successful businesses. He was a very smart person and much sought after for his advice. Her mother was "Mrs. Volunteer" for every charity in the community.

Barbara was expected to carry on the family traditions. Not a problem with her. She actually looked forward to it. As such, she was taking business courses just as I was. We were both dating other people at the time. Truth be known, I was dating two girls at the same time, until they found out about each other. Then, oh boy, hell hath no fury.... Barbara was dating one guy she seemed pretty serious about. He was the son of the town's outstanding doctor. I think they planned to marry, but you know about plans. Rumor was, she caught him with another girl, and I do mean "caught." Barbara had fire. She was almost arrested for attacking them, but the charges were dropped.

DeEarlon

It was several months before either of us went out with anyone again. She wouldn't even talk to another guy. Slowly, very slowly, we started to talk to each other about problems and assignments in school. After a few months, we were at least comfortable with each other.

Then I made a major mistake. I asked her out. It was like you hit her with a brick. She was shocked and insulted. She just turned away and didn't talk to me for two weeks. That's it, I thought. This beautiful, raven-haired goddess is through with me.

Then, right out of nowhere, she marched up to me one night after class and said, "Okay, let's go out."

Now I was shocked. Later, I was almost sorry after the first date. Truly, I had an icicle next to me all that evening. But I was polite. I didn't even try to give her a peck on the cheek when I dropped her off after the date.

Next class, just a "hello" from her.

Class after that, "Would you like to go out again, Jim?"

Just like that, cold and machine-like. I really wasn't sure, but Barbara was a stunningly beautiful girl. So I said yes. An hour into the date, she was all over me. You just can't figure women.

Though I try to remember, the next few months and years are mostly a blur, but a good blur. We dated all the way through to graduation, the next two years. Then we got married.

*

Phinng – dumph. Sniper! The shot hit the stump. I hunker down deeper and hold my breath.

*

So there we were, married. I got a job in the credit department of a large appliance store, and she got a job in the human resources department of a bank. We started making pretty good money between us. Living in a small, third-floor apartment, we were able to start saving for a house. We were still young, so we had our problems and disagreements, but we stuck it out. I think we learned to respect each other a lot.

One day we had a big disagreement. I don't remember what it was about, but it was the aftermath that was important. We made up, and made up again. A few weeks after this making up, she told me she was expecting. That changed things. If you weren't grown up already, you grew up fast. It was a girl. We named her Rachael, and she was the cutest little package on earth! Of course, I'm being completely impartial here.

Okay, married with child. It's time we got a house. With our mediocre savings and help from her parents, we bought a place. A nice house in a nice neighborhood, it wasn't new, and it needed a few repairs, but that brought the price down a little. We were in the system, and happy to be there.

Homeowners with child, for the first time. I started paying attention to politics for the first time. Shortly after moving in, we received invitations from both major political parties to join them. Both, of course, claimed to be the true representatives of the people and the people's important interests. My father-in-law had his own opinions on politics but, to his credit, told us we must make up our own minds. As I said, a smart man.

Our new neighbor, Pete, was an old libertarian and advised us not to join any political party. Not knowing what to do, I did nothing…for too long, as it turned out.

Accordingly, I missed the first election in our community, and I didn't care. I didn't care until I got the first notice of a major tax increase on our home.

"Increase for what?" I bellowed.

Where are the improvements to justify this? They would know my wrath, I vowed. As such, I strutted into the next town council meeting, full of fury, and pledging to clip their wings. Standing at the podium, full of fire and brimstone, my demands were simple.

"What are you people spending so much money on?"

DeEarlon

The reaction throughout the council chamber surprised me. It was simple, low laughter, from both sides.

One councilman looked at me and asked, "Don't you read what's going on in town, sir?" I had not. Having no real answer, I slunk away red-faced. It was a long time before I attended another meeting.

After a few weeks, I finally mustered the courage to ask Pete about town expenses. Aside from the usual ones, which he thought exorbitant to begin with, he mentioned the situation with the town library. It seemed that the library flooded every other year because it was located next to a large stream.

"Well," I foolishly asked, "Why don't they just dam the stream?"

"Can't do that," Pete replied. "Army Corps of Engineers and environmental department won't let yah." With that, Pete went into a long, complex explanation of why you couldn't dam the stream or move the library.

I was overwhelmed by the tangled interplay of government agencies, laws and red tape Pete described. I knew business was complicated, but I really didn't think politics, particularly on a small, suburban level, would be that complex.

The shock of learning how much we were directly controlled by the federal government bowled me over. During the next few years, I was in for an education in government, a very depressing education.

*

"Jim, how you doing here? Still holding this section of the line, I see."

Paul had arrived, snapping me back to the present.

"For a while, Paul. Hey buddy, you'd better keep your head a little lower while you've still got one."

"Yeah, I know. Believe me," he halted a minute. "I still remember Al. Hey, where's Tom? Did he move down a few yards to cover?"

I flipped my thumb backwards. He looked into the shade of the thick brush behind me.

"Oh, God," Paul sighed, crossing himself and tightening his jaw. "We lost a lot in the last attack, Jim. I don't know if we can hold. I've been polling guys, oh, and some of our gals, to see if they want to fall back and tighten ranks. We're getting kinda thin on the line."

"Paul, what does it matter? You heard their tanks move up. It's best if we're farther apart when they fire. Fewer killed when their shells hit. By the way, you got any ammo?"

"Hell, Jim, nobody has any ammo. The next assault will probably be it. I don't know why the feds just don't bring in some fighter jets to finish us, the bastards."

"Why waste the fuel? Those jets take a lot. Fuel is expensive! The government guys need it for their limos, Paul."

We both laughed a little.

"Okay Jim, I've got to move on down the line. Oh, General Ordway says to prepare for the next assault about 13:00 hours."

Paul hesitated, glancing back.

"You don't have to tell your men."

He started to move out, stopped, then reached back, right hand extended.

"Been a pleasure knowing you, Jim."

"Same here, Paul."

We clasped hands hard for a second before he moved on. Watching him for a moment, I took a swig from my canteen, and fell back against the stump.

*

Barb was damned mad. Between the fiasco at the town council meeting and Pete's explanation of how government worked in town, she almost exploded. My wife has a temper.

I catch myself. My wife *had* a temper. She said we had to get involved so we could change things. I agreed, but didn't know how. Old Pete was well versed in local and state politics, but he was more of a complainer than a doer. There are times, though, when fate intervenes.

I was in front of our house one day, trimming weeds. Looking up, I saw a man walking briskly down the street; damned if it wasn't one of the town councilman. It turned out he often took long, brisk walks to help eliminate his middle-aged spread. His name was John Barret, and he was an institution because his ancestors helped settle the place, and because he was about to become the longest-serving councilman in town history, eleven two-year terms.

Amazingly, he recognized me.

"Hello there, young man. You were the one at the council meeting a few months ago. Your name is ahh..."

"James, sir. James Lamberti."

"Oh yes, yes. Some fire in you, James, but it needs direction. Why don't you come to one of our party meetings next Tuesday night at town hall? We'd be happy to see you, and you might start getting the direction you need."

"Thank you, Mr. Barret, but I don't belong to your party. Fact is, I don't belong to any party."

"That's your problem right there, James. You don't belong to a party! I'll tell you a little secret about politics and government, James. If you don't belong to a party, you'll never get anything done. You have to work from within the system to accomplish anything," he said.

"Take old Pete, your neighbor. You must know by now that he's a chronic complainer. He complains about everything, and some of his complaints are good and justified. But Pete never accomplishes anything because he won't join a party. You get nothing done alone, Jim. Nothing."

"I'll think about it, Mr. Barret."

"Please, call me John." He laughed. "Nobody calls me Mr.

The Revolutionist

Barret!" He slapped me on the back and continued on his way. Looking back, he hollered, "See you next Tuesday, Jim!"

After I finished my yard work, I went in and told Barbara what had happened.

*

THARUMP. Artillery fire. A short, screeching whistle, then a deep, sharp *BOOM*, and the earth exploded as dirt, mud and rock were hurled twenty feet into the air, right behind our berm, down 150 yards to my left.

I heard a man's agonized cry. Mercifully, his shrieks lasted only a few seconds. We all listened for more fire, but there was only silence. They were toying with us again. They were letting us know they had the power, and that we'd better think about it. But there was nothing to think about. The luxury of surrender had passed a long time before.

Smoke from the explosion passes over me a few seconds later in almost psychedelic swirls. Smoke. The reek of white phosphorus and death.

*

John Barret stood outside the town hall's main entrance as Barb and I approached. He was puffing on a huge cigar, and swirls of smoke surrounded him.

"Glad you could make it, Jim. And this is?"

"Oh, Mr. Barret, this is my wife, Barbara. Barbara, this is John Barret, the councilman I told you about."

Barbara nodded politely. She hated the smell of cigars and would go no closer to Barret.

"So good to see both of you! We need young people in government. So few participate these days, and that's the crux of the problem. We especially need good-looking young women. You lucky dog, you, Jim. Ha ha! Come on, let's go in."

He turned, and Barbara rolled her eyes. Barret guided us

through the front doors, down the hall, and into the main council chamber. He sat us close to where his own seat was, at one end of the line of council members.

"You two stay right here and I'll try, when I can, to let you know what's going on and why."

Barret turned away to talk to others entering the large room. Many of them looked our way questioningly.

That was the moment. You know, there's always that moment. Yes, that was definitely it. I wasn't in a political party yet, and I certainly wasn't in government, but it didn't matter. For the first time, I felt I was a part of government. A tiny part of the great wheel that made our country function. It was a good moment, and though I didn't show it, way down deep, I was excited.

Later that night, long after we got home, Barb said she'd felt the same way. It was contagious and powerful.

Within the month, we'd both become members of the Conservative Party and joined the Conservative Town Committee. At first, the commitment in time was just a day or two a month. Our new endeavor was exciting, fun and uplifting. We felt like we were truly contributing. We became well known, and we were invited to all sorts of affairs, official and private, from both major parties. New friends and acquaintances flooded our world.

Then, slowly, reality began to sink in. Conservatives were indeed a major party, but not *the* major party. They were tolerated by voters, but the truth was, the Progressive Party ruled the roost. Nothing, and I mean nothing, happened in town without the blessing of the Progressives. This was driven home one day by what came to be known as the Hemple Affair.

*

Shots. Three in a row, and they snapped me out of my daydreams. I grabbed my rifle and whirled around to peer over the top of my protective stump. Nothing! No federal attack. No more shots. On both sides of me, comrades were doing the same.

A low but growing noise came down the line. It finally reached my ears: "Shots fired in prep. Prepare to repel advance." I passed it on.

The thought struck me: Our line is pitifully thin. The distance between me and the men of either side is at least fifteen yards, maybe more. If there's a full frontal assault, we'll fold.

It's then that I meet Gil.

"How you doin', Sergeant? Reporting as ordered!"

He was a kid. He'd come crawling along the line from the north, dragging his rifle. No, truly, a kid! If he was sixteen, it was a miracle.

"I'm one of the recruits. Name is Gil, Sergeant Lamberti. I'm here to help reinforce your position. They also told me to give you this."

He reached into his jacket and pulled out a thirty-round ammo magazine. Wow, I was up to 100 rounds now!

"Why are you here, kid?"

"Told you, Sergeant, to help reinforce the line."

"How old are you?"

"I'm gonna be seventeen next month."

"I say again, why are you here, kid?"

"To help reinforce...."

"Okay, stop. Where's your family? They let you come here?"

The kid, Gil, suddenly looked down.

"My mother - don't know - probably killed in a gas attack by the feds," he slowly said. "My father and older brother...shot in front of me last year. The goddam feds held me. They were going to send me to a re-education camp because I was only fifteen."

Gil looked at me. "So I took off. Made it to the woods before they could shoot me. They were too busy to follow, but they bombed the woods later. There were ten or twelve of us hiding out there. Five made it through the bombing. Six days later, we met a rebel patrol. They took us to their camp.

"I trained. I've already been in combat, Sergeant. I ain't no damn virgin. I got at least five or six of 'em at the Roanoke action last month. I loved my family, and those bastards are gonna pay."

He fell silent, shifting to the other side of the stump.

"Okay, Gil. Welcome to rebel base central."

I held out my hand. He just nodded. A minute later, he reached into his jacket.

"Want a cigarette? I got a couple left."

"Hey, Gil, those things'll kill you."

We both laughed. Then we leaned against the stump and lit up, waiting.

*

Old Art Hemple, I remembered him. He and his wife lived about two blocks from Barb and me. I didn't know the man well, but everyone in town knew of him from parades and other civic events. He was one of the guys - no - he was *the* guy at the front of every parade. He was a war veteran who always held the flag high and marched in center-front of all the other veterans. Hemple was the proudest of the proud when it came to his service to the country.

Although at least 75, not one of the other vets, regardless of age, could step off a march stronger or faster than him.

The Hemples, both of them, were favorites with all the kids in the neighborhood. Mrs. Hemple baked tons of cookies of every sort at least twice a week. She passed them out to all the kids who stopped by the house. And why did they all stop by the Hemple household? To hear Hemple read children's stories to them on the back porch, of course! The Hemples were a legend in town, and a good one.

Then, the new ordinance was passed.

I didn't attend every council meeting. I didn't have to, I wasn't on the council. But it was at one of our Conservative Town Committee meetings that we all saw John Barret more upset than almost anyone had ever seen him before.

The vote had been 6 to 3. Six Progressive votes for, and three Conservative votes against. The new ordinance forbade most displays of the American flag. Flags two by three feet or larger could not be displayed on any day expect the Fourth of July, and then only by special permit. Larger flags were said to be "disruptive" in nature and could possibly be an insult to many new immigrants to our country.

Hey, if they wanted to be in our country, they should be proud of our flag, I thought. If they weren't proud of our flag, why were they in our country, and what was the problem with our own citizens?

Barret reported that harsh words had flown during the council meeting, and bad feelings were permanently implanted. The Progressives weren't about to let some silly old patriotism get in the way of their ideas.

Hemple had a large, four by six-foot American flag on permanent display on a tall pole in front of his house. He raised it every morning and lowered it every sunset, according to proper protocol.

About a week after the ordinance passed, Hemple received a letter from the town. It ordered him to take the flag down. Of course, Hemple promptly ignored the order. A few days later, the zoning enforcement officer paid him a visit. Hemple threw him off the property.

The next morning, a police car with two officers pulled up to the Hemple house, only to be greeted by Hemple himself in his old Army uniform. They ordered him to stand down and back away from the pole so they could lower the flag. Hemple refused, shouting that they were traitors, whereupon they tased him. Before they even checked on the man, sprawled on the ground and shaking, they hauled the flag down, crumpled it, then threw it in the police car's trunk.

Finally they checked Hemple. He wasn't breathing. The police called an ambulance, but by the time the ambulance transported him to a hospital, Hemple was dead.

That sent the town into an uproar. A large group of veterans, led by Mrs. Hemple, attempted to storm the next town council meeting. They were met outside by the police and told to go home. Councilman Barret told the police to let them pass, whereupon he was arrested for interfering with the police. The police chief and several patrolmen later apologized privately to Barret.

They only did what they were ordered to do, they said. But again, the Progressives had proven their power, and I got my first, hard lesson in the cancer slowly infecting our country: A country I once thought the fairest in all the world.

Chapter Two - Pa.

The once clear, blue skies clouded over and a light mist filled the air. Light or not, the mist soaked us. Gil didn't have a rain poncho, so I went back, took Tom's and gave it to Gil. I apologized to Tom.

It was well past the time the feds were supposed to attack. Messages passed back and forth and indicated confusion. At 19:00 hours, we were ordered to stand down. Someone said there was intelligence that the attack had been aborted. At that point, it really didn't matter. It was pure anticlimax.

The good part was that, shortly after that, a low, flat wagon pulled by two guys, virtually crawling, came along. It was a wagon full of food! Command had finally found us some decent chow. Everyone got a freeze-dried dinner, no choice in what you got, and some sort of flavored water. The water was better than the dinner, but you know - any port in a storm. I think they requisitioned this stuff from some old grocery store that was, well, old. But it did fill an empty belly.

We ate slowly because this gave the illusion of more food, and because we had nothing else to do. Gil needed no advice from me on slow eating. That tended to confirm his story about being a veteran despite his age.

When finished, we savored our fruit-flavored water. I wished it was something stronger than water. Gil wished he had more cigarettes. Then we fell silent for a few minutes, until I asked him about the events that led him here.

Gil leaned back, a far-away look on his face. That face proved he'd been through hell and back. Despite his youth, it was the face of an old man.

"Some other time, Sergeant," he said. He started field stripping and cleaning his weapon.

I'd already cleaned mine twice that day. I figured it really didn't need to be cleaned again. Better to keep it ready for action. So what do you do when there's nothing else to do? You remember.

*

I remembered the next meeting of the Conservative Town Committee; it was a hot one. It had been a long time since some of the members were that worked up. We voted to hire a lawyer, but when we checked the committee budget, we amended that vote to a resolution to search for one who would work "pro bono": free.

That made some members laugh and others angry. How would we ever get a good attorney for free? Remember, they said, we're talking about lawyers here. But we did get one, and it was because of Barbara. Back in school she'd been friendly with a young law student who needed some business courses. When Barb called her, she agreed to represent us, mostly, I think, because she had no other clients. Her name was Joan Bleu, and she was smart and ambitious, but she was also young and untried in the fires of politics and the courts.

Joan met with our committee to decide what issue to tackle first. Did we go after the size-of-the-flag issue first, or being locked out of a town council meeting? It was decided almost unanimously that being locked out of a public town meeting by the decision of another political party was definitely the larger issue. We could address the flag ordinance later.

What happened next was crushing, but not just for our community. Attorney Joan Bleu filed our suit, only to have the state court refuse to hear it because we had "no standing"! She filed another, slightly amended suit, only to have that one denied. Three more suits were filed and all denied on various trivial grounds.

The message to us was sinking in. Worse, we learned that similar situations were occurring all over the country. People, common people, were beginning to get angry at their own government; a government that had been, if not loved, at least always respected throughout our history. Many had lain down their lives for this form of government and our way of life.

What was happening now, as we looked across our land, truly shocked and sickened us. Joan was at her wits' end, and was virtually out of money.

It started small, but began to grow; the quiet chant of "something isn't right here, and something must be done."

Barbara was revved. She took over recruiting new members for our town committee while simultaneously speaking to voters of the other party about, if not actually changing political allegiance, at least voting for new, honest people. My assignment from Barbara was to go to the state capital with John Barret and make some noise about honest government, then investigate the integrity of the state courts.

The late Art Hemple, and now his widow, Mrs. Hemple, became our poster martyrs. Torrent doesn't begin to describe the amount of publicity we got. When the next election day rolled around, we thought we had a lock on our town council. When the numbers came in, they were close, but we were ahead, and we maintained that lead well into the next morning.

Barret went to the council chambers that morning to demand a concession from the Progressives, who had been mysteriously quiet until now. That's when lightning struck.

*

My young friend broke my train of thought.

"Sergeant! You awake?" Gil leaned over and shook my arm.

"Guess I dozed off for a minute," I replied groggily. Then I instinctively grabbed my rifle. "We under attack?"

"No attack. But I've just been up for over 20 hours now and could really use some sleep."

"Sure," I yawned. "Get some shuteye, kid. If anything happens, you'll be the first to know."

I smiled, and Gil rolled up into a ball.

Sighing again, my memory searched back to where I'd left off. Just as the thoughts formed again, a helicopter thrumped fast and low over our position, and there was shouting everywhere.

It was definitely a fed spy chopper. Just as my instinct caused me to hunker down, a rocket from our lines split the black night sky. The chopper's rotors burst into a bright balloon of yellow and red as the craft banked left, too late. Now the flaming machine slammed into the no-man's land between the lines, and an even larger explosion lit up the landscape for a mile in all directions.

I laughed to myself. The bastards thought we were out of rockets. Obviously, we weren't. Gil slept right through it.

*

You could hear Barret's shout all the way down the main corridor at town hall. Several more screams assaulted our ears before he came charging out of council chambers toward us.

"You're not going to believe this! They claim they won! They claim they found 600 uncounted votes in the bottom of a voting machine, votes for them, of course!"

Pandemonium broke out in our group, with some screaming, some cursing and others struck silent.

Joan Bleu erupted. "That's it! I'm taking this to the state election commission."

One town committee member erupted back, "Why bother? The handwriting's on the wall."

At that moment, many just gave up and walked away, from election politics at least. A kind of dark, inner hardness was born at that moment. A bitterness began to grow. As we all returned home and saw the local election results from across the country, the bitterness only grew deeper. Our situation was echoed in dozens of states and communities nationwide. The shadow seemed to deepen and spread. There was a tightness in the gut that never really let up.

The Revolutionist

"Jim, we'll get all the members we can and descend on the state legislature." Barbara was adamant. "We'll make such a noise...."

"Don't bother." Barret, the old soldier, appeared exhausted. "Don't you see what you're up against? This wasn't just an election, it was a turning point. Even if they don't get the votes, they will find ways of winning. They now control elections," Barret warned.

"Consider the wave of illegal immigrants being allowed into our country. Look, I have as much compassion as anyone, certainly more than those two-faced Progressives. But these people are actually destroying our country. Most are illiterate or they have another language and an entirely different culture. They're changing the way our nation functions, and not for the better."

Barret sank into a chair in the corridor.

"They'll be allowed to vote, and they'll only vote one way; not for traditional America. In the meantime, legal citizens have to support them at enormous cost. Many middle-income people are being pulled into a lower economic class by the taxes they have to pay to support these illegals, who will never politically support the middle class they're destroying.

"The Progressives have found a way to have our citizens destroy themselves."

According to Barrett, we were all witnesses to the perfect murder plot.

"And those who live through the murder will be poorer, second-class citizens in their own country. Why bother to vote anymore?"

He spat, he actually spat, on the floor, clenched his jaw and walked away.

Over the next few months, dozens of citizens attended the town council meetings, thinking their just anger could and would make a difference. They were wrong, and though many meetings ended in shouts and threats, nothing changed. Except for John Barret, who was still trying, the Conservative Party leaders wimped out. They made a few speeches in protest, but little else.

Many formerly involved citizens dropped out of local government in disgust, but a few began paying closer attention to affairs locally and nationally. They didn't like what they saw developing. This smaller group was determined to fight on and do more than the spineless Conservatives dared do.

Barbara and I belonged to the latter group.

I seem to recall that we limped along for a few months, trying to meet people and get them involved. It was a discouraging time. You met someone, had them over, heard their complaints. But when you asked them to do anything, they begged off. Damn!

Fate surprises you at times, though.

We were having a little get together of family and close friends to announce the news. Our little daughter, Rachael, was going to be a big sister! Barb was glowing. It was the happiest she had been in a couple of years.

We invited Joan Bleu to the party. In the time we'd known her, we had become close. It was during that party that Joan took me aside to say she wanted me to meet a certain professor she knew. He was a professor of political science, and she wanted our group to meet him. She didn't want to bother Barbara right then in her moment of joy, so she was only mentioning it to me.

"Sure, we'd love to hear what he has to say, Joan," I said.

"He's controversial, Jim. He's a big critic of the government and the way things are developing in this country."

"And we aren't?" I replied. We both snickered.

"No, I mean really controversial. He's writing a book about how bad this government is and what the people can do about it. It's almost, well, he could be wearing a tri-cornered hat, if you know what I mean."

"Where's my musket?" I joked. Again, we chuckled.

We sauntered over to John Barret and set up a preliminary time when, if this professor agreed, he could speak before the Conservative Town Committee.

"Joan, what's his name?" Barret asked.

"Professor Phillip Athenson."

*

"Just before dawn. That's what they said, Sergeant."

Now it was my turn to thank Gil. I was the sleepyhead this time, and I'd drifted into a deep slumber while reminiscing. Technically, I could be shot for sleeping on watch. It endangered not only Gil and me, but our position and our entire force.

I say "technically" because I'm sure three quarters of our troops were asleep that night, including most of those who were supposed to be on watch. We'd had a rough few days. Then too, if they shot all who dozed, it would be a big loss. There weren't that many of us left.

Still trying to shake the sleep from my foggy brain, I asked Gil, "When did they come through, and were there any orders?"

"About ten minutes ago. I was gonna wake you, but I was awake, so I let you sleep. It was your buddy, Paul, and a small supply wagon. The whole news package was kinda' mixed. They said they have reliable intel that government forces are going to attack at 04:50 hours, while it's still dark. That's in about fifteen minutes. They want to hit us with some enormous spotlights so they can blind us."

"The only way you can repel a force then is to blanket fire into the light. That's a lot of ammo, and we don't have much left," I replied.

"Actually, we do, Sergeant." Gil smiled.

He lifted something and handed it to me. It was four thirty-round magazines.

"In fact, they were full of good news," Gil added. "During the night, we got resupplied with a huge load of ammo, rockets and thermite grenades. When those tanks advance, we'll melt 'em.'"

I was about to speak, but Gil held up his hand.

"Sorry, Sergeant, but there's more!"

He produced some sort of large, wrapped bar - food - and a foam cup that smelled like coffee. I took the cup, ripped the top off and gulped. It was still warm. I was in heaven!

I saved a little coffee, devoured the bar, then finished the coffee. My bladder began to scream, so I crawled over into the bushes behind us. While there, my nose told me that my old friend, Tom Neil, needed to be buried. As I put my equipment away, I apologized to Tom again.

"Sorry Tom, there just isn't time now. I'm so sorry."

Freezing in place for a second, a single tear rolled down my cheek. Was it for me or for Tom? I wiped it away quickly and crawled back toward Gil and the line. As I returned, Gil excused himself for the same reason. Checking my watch, we had slightly over six minutes before showtime. A deep sigh, and I reentered my memories.

*

"And I tell you, they are bastardizing our nation. This is not what we were set up to be. This is not the hope of all humanity that we came so close to becoming."

I was stirred. I was truly stirred by this Phillip Athenson. As I looked around the room, everyone was transfixed. Barbara had tears in her eyes, and John Barret was hyperventilating. This was exactly what our committee needed. Then I glanced down for a minute and thought, this is what our nation needs. This man has the power to remind us of why we became a nation in the first place.

As Athenson talked, heads nodded. He talked of the complete incompetence in Washington; of the withdrawal of our troops in foreign lands only to have those lands collapse, turn and threaten us; of high unemployment or underemployment; of the wild inflation of our money, only to have prices rise sharply; of the forced purchase of medical insurance, lower prices promised, higher prices resulting.

He spoke of the invasion of our nation by countless people over our southern border, our resources strained to the breaking point to care for them while nothing was done to stop this seemingly endless influx. Humane, perhaps, but certainly nation-breaking.

Athenson checked off every major problem our country had. Almost all these problems originated in our nation's capital, and most of those were created by the present administration, but without one of them being solved by them.

The media, he said, were intimately complicit in these crimes for either under-reporting them or not reporting them at all. And crimes they were, he continued, because so many violated the Constitution, our supreme law. Further, who would bring charges for these crimes?

"Ha, there be the rub. Neither Congress nor the worthless attorney general will hold the president responsible for breaking the law and virtually assuming dictatorial powers," Athenson stated. "Before our eyes, before our very eyes, the nation that we and our forebears worked so hard to establish and build is being torn apart. It must be stopped."

We all broke into wild applause. Everywhere this man spoke, crowds cheered. It was the turning of a nation. But that seemed to be a problem for those in power.

John Barret was too involved to notice a new guest during Athenson's speech, but I wasn't. Sauntering over to this possible new committee member, I introduced myself. He seemed surprised for a split second, then replied.

"Oh yeah. I'm Mike Paine. Nice to meet you."

That's it, that's all he said, but I continued.

"Are you new in town?"

"No, no. Actually I'm just passing through." He turned away

for a moment, then turned back to me. "Yeah, ah, what's your name again?"

I told him, then asked how he knew about this meeting.

"A friend told me."

I asked who, and Paine said he'd forgotten.

"Forgot?" I fired back.

"Hey buddy, I gotta go."

He started to leave and I grabbed his arm.

"I wouldn't do that, friend, not unless you want real trouble," he growled.

I let go and he rushed out. Immediately, I went over to Barret and told him what had happened.

"I guess you just met one, Jim."

"One what?' I replied.

"A government spy. The government doesn't like Athenson, or anyone who likes Athenson. You know, like us, people who still believe in freedom."

"Oh, come on, John, this is the United States of America. Things like that...."

Barret held up a hand. "Stop, Jim. I'll take you over to talk to Athenson later. You have a lot to learn about how this country has changed in the last few years." My naiveté was beginning to fade.

I remember meeting Professor Athenson at the end of that committee session. He wasn't young, perhaps sixty-five, but neither was he old. Truly, Athenson was one of those who attained an awe-inspiring maturity, but never age. He exuded a vitality and strength men half his age don't have.

When I told him about Paine, Athenson smirked.

"Get used to it people, get used to it. They routinely spy on any of us they consider even remotely not in their camp. And when our imagined transgressions become too flagrant, as in my case, they will attempt to destroy you, one way or another. Truly, steel yourselves for what is about to come."

The Revolutionist

I couldn't believe what I was hearing!

*

"FLARES - FLARES!" The shout went up and down the line. I snapped back to consciousness and grabbed for my rifle. No rifle! I panicked for a second, until I noticed it had just fallen over. Picking it up, my gaze shifted to Gil.

"You almost got a foot to the butt, Sergeant," he said. "Damn, you dream a lot."

That was as far as our conversation went, as mortar shells blew right behind our lines on the berm, the perfect fire control almost certainly due to silent fed drones. We lost a lot more guys. It was a slaughter.

Gil and I were lucky, probably not in a spot with enough armed resistance to waste a mortar round on, at least not in the first attack. A second barrage hit. The two guys immediately to our right disappeared in a sudden wall of roaring, smoking dirt, and that's when my right ear drum went.

A third barrage hit, this one at least fifty yards behind us. What the hell were they aiming at?

"They're comin'!" someone screamed.

Small arms fire filled the air. Without thinking, Gil and I popped our rifles over the berm and started firing blindly. A few seconds later, we cautiously raised our heads high enough to see what, if anything, we were firing at. We saw.

Directly in front of us, about fifty yards away, was a mass of enemy – government -- soldiers, at least seventy to 100 headed right for us. Firing directly at them, we hit a lot, but they were all wearing body armor. We dented the line, but it didn't stop.

Something happens when you're in battle. Yes, there's terror, a fear that can make you freeze. Then your adrenalin kicks in, sweeping everything away except an angry numbness. All else is forgotten, and you force yourself to move.

I fired directly at those closing in. Gil went down for a

second. When he came up, he had some sort of cloth-wrapped package in his hand. He heaved it mightily into the largest pod of approaching belligerents. Within a second, there was a large, muffled explosion and a brilliant white flash. Ten or twelve went down immediately, and a like number around them also went down - slowly. Gil resumed fire, backing me up.

We held them for a minute until some of our own mortar fire blew large holes in their approaching line. They stopped and, after a second or two, incredibly, they retreated!

I fell back against my old friend, the stump. I was exhausted. The action only lasted for ten or twelve minutes, but it felt like hours. All of it, all this nightmare, was catching up with me. Sometimes I felt it was time to take a bullet - and rest; leave all this shit behind. Soon enough, I thought; soon enough. My eyes drifted over toward Gil.

"Hey, buddy, was that package you tossed what I think it was?"

"Yeah, Sarge, it was a thermite grenade. I learned that trick even before Roanoke. You spread a cloth or a bag or whatever, fill it with pebbles or nails -- whatever you got -- and put a grenade in it. Then you wrap it up tight, pull the pin and toss it. It increases the power of the grenade by ten."

Gil was still peeping nervously over the berm top.

"All we got is the thermites," he continued. "I hate to waste 'em, but we had to use something. If the tanks come, we only got two thermites left, but that's life."

Then he laughed. "Or I hope it is." He slumped down, staring blankly into the brush behind us.

"Gil, how did your family get mixed up in all this?"

He didn't answer for a minute. Then, without looking up, "Guess like everybody else. We got mad at the government. My mom and dad really hated that Washington was taking more and more power to itself and just runnin' over people and their rights."

Gil explained that his father had been a labor union official, a shop steward.

"But, you know, he thought power should be in the hands of the people, for themselves. Not in the hands of a few big wigs in the capital tellin' us what to do every day. When the trouble started, Washington expected all the union members to back them up. Those that didn't..."

He broke off.

"Not all the union members backed those bastards, did they, Sergeant?"

"No they didn't, Gil."

"Bastards!" Then he stopped talking and just stared.

The sun was coming up. You could see the tortured, pock-marked landscape now.

*

As I listened to Professor Athenson, what I learned shocked me.

"Consider the word 'totalitarianism.' What it means is that the government totally controls your life. Totally. At one time this country and its people opposed this concept, but look at our nation today. The government tells children what they can study and eat in school, tells businesses largely what they can do and who they can hire, where your home can be and every aspect of life within your home, what you can drive or even if you *can* drive. They tell you that you must buy health insurance and what kind of insurance they will let you buy, whether you're allowed to protect yourself or not, who you can associate with and who you can't, even -- through intimidation -- what you can think.

"I ask you in all honestly, is that not totalitarianism? They're one tiny step from controlling your entire life. And as to your life, they tell you to die early, please, and lessen the strain on the rest of us."

Athenson sighed.

"Freedom? Where is it? Oh, and be very careful what you say

about this situation, or else you're in trouble."

"Professor, professor!" A middle aged man from the audience waved his hand. "You won't believe this. Last fall some siding blew off my house. I picked it all up and was in the process of reattaching it when the building inspector showed up. He said I needed a permit to put my own siding back on, and, I couldn't do it myself. I had to have a licensed contractor do it! This is *my* house and I can't do something like that? I told him to get lost and the town sued me. I had to hire a lawyer. The whole process cost me over $2,500 plus the cost of the contractor. My own house for something this small. Unbelievable!"

"Exactly sir. You have just experienced the end of private property. Government at every level now tells us what to do with our own property. In effect, there is no more private property. It's all government land, and you rent from them," Athenson said.

"Remember this, private property is the very backbone of a free society; or used to be. And have you noticed who they go after to advance their 'total' agenda. They always go after those who can't defend themselves, the old or the sick, those who have to work for a living, or the small homeowner and the small business owner who must work constantly. These people have neither the time nor the money to go up against the government," he added.

"Then who agrees with them? Who goes into the streets and shouts and riots, demanding 'reform,' as long as that reform can be controlled by the government? These are the chronically unemployed, and happy to be that way; the 'professional' students, and devoted leftists from all walks of life. Most who don't care what you want, need or dream of. They're happy to glide on the government's dime, which is actually 'your' dime - and dollar, taken from you by excessive taxation and 'fees'."

Whether you agree or disagree with the government and its representatives, Athenson explained, "one thing you expect from them is adherence to the law. I mean, these guys make the

The Revolutionist

laws. It's their own rules. So when they flagrantly break those rules, and disregard the nation's and the peoples' welfare at the same time, for their own purposes, it's criminal," he said.

"Consider,. We have a Constitution. That Constitution, any constitution, is a supreme law. Let me repeat that, our supreme law. ALL - ALL other laws in this country must comply with our Constitution or such laws are themselves illegal. To make matters worse, we have a Supreme Court that now routinely says our president and his minions are right in what they do, regardless of the Constitution. History, my friends, shows us clearly that when a society violates its own rules and long-successful political traditions, that nation is headed in only one direction: the garbage heap of history."

I had never looked at it that way. We all knew there weren't a lot of people who were happy with our oh-so-perfect leaders. Nobody likes being told what to buy, and business didn't like be told how to run their own show. It didn't take a genius to see that all this led to higher unemployment.

Athenson said, though, that's what they wanted: Unemployment or under employment so we'd all be dependent on the government for life and necessities. Then he talked about how they used the power to tax to intimidate their opposition.

After that night, we became devoted followers of the good professor. A lot of us became volunteers. Some of us went house to house with fliers, and some of us spoke at different places when invited. One thing I noticed: Folks started to divide into two distinct camps, the "governmentals" and the "hell no, we've had enough-ers."

It shouldn't have been like that, not here; but it was. The more I thought about it, it made my stomach turn. This was my country, my proud refuge. And it wasn't just in our town, it was all across the land.

One day Barb and I got a notice from our health insurance company that, per federal government regulation, our old health policy was voided. The new one, required by law, they said, would raise our rates 25 percent, and our deductible was going up to $1,800. I was furious. When I called to complain, they said there was nothing they could do, it was the law now.

You sit and you fume; and you fume until it moves you to action.

The day finally came, Barb had a miscarriage. It was bad, both physically and mentally for her. Our local hospital emergency room was packed, and when we called our doctor, we were told he'd been dropped from our company's coverage. I had to drive her to the emergency room of a small hospital forty miles away. By the time she got care, Barb was out of it mentally and there was significant physical damage. We were told afterward that she might never be able to have a natural birth again. Oh, and for that wonderful information, it cost us $1,400 out of pocket.

A few days later, when I was sure Barb was reasonably okay, , I visited our local federal building. Storming into the health and welfare office, I really let them have it.

Then they let me have it. Two police officers, on permanent duty there, told me to back off at once or I'd be placed under arrest.

"Arrest for what?" I bellowed.

They silently glared. Biting my tongue, and still shaking with fury, I backed out of the office. Angry or not, I'm no fool.

My next stop was our newspaper office. After I told them what had happened, they just shrugged. It turned out they agreed with Washington and all the changes. Sam Minton, managing editor, said it was about time that government started governing.

"Not like this, and not here!" I retorted.

"Oh, we think it should be even stronger. And not here? People need to be guided, molded and controlled," Minton said, and just stared at me.

Open-mouthed, I turned to go, then I turned back with a smart remark I'd just thought of.

The Revolutionist

Minton was gone - poof. Did you ever see one of those old movies where the guy keeps living some nightmare over and over? That's just how I felt. Fear began to creep in. Where was my country, that great, fair, free land, and where were all the brave, fair people in it and defending it?

As I walked back to my car, I felt myself shaking again. But this time it wasn't fury.

Chapter Three - N.J.

It was hot, and it wasn't even noon yet. I glanced at my watch: 11:32 a.m. and the temperature had to be 90 degrees. The smell of human sweat, mixed with the growing stench of death, filled the air. Even the water in my canteen, which I kept out of the sun, was like warm tea. A normal person would get sick under these conditions, but I guess it's really true that you get used to anything.

Another long sigh. Boredom. Constant boredom, depression and anxiety all plagued me.

"Gil, did they assign you to this unit?"

"No, Sarge, I volunteered."

"Did they tell you about this unit? How it was probably singled out for 'special treatment' by the feds?"

"Yeah, they did. That's why so many volunteered."

I looked directly at Gil. "Are you...are you all crazy? The feds want to annihilate everyone in this unit. That crap they throw out about parading rebels who give up in front of the cameras so it proves how humane and forgiving they are. That doesn't apply to this unit, if it really applies to any. They actually told you about us?"

"I said yes, Sarge. In fact, that's why so many volunteered. This unit is special to every reb out there. You guys are our idols. You're the guys who set the example. You're the ones who got into the capital - in force - just after the revolution started and got the big bastards. You guys actually arrested, tried, convicted, and hung the head of the senate, the damn thief; the attorney general, who refused to indict criminals; and the head of the IRS, the president's personal hit man. Every real patriot loves you guys and wants to be part of this unit."

"Gil, you must realize that's why there will be no mercy for this unit if the rebellion fails."

The Revolutionist

Sometimes things just hit you out of the blue. Not having much time to think about this before, the real reason came to me.

"That's why, Gil. That's why they aren't hitting us with nukes or gas or whatever. They're actually trying to capture as many of us alive as possible."

I bit my lower lip.

"Then they'll make a terrible example of us being executed. It's not going to be pretty, kid."

"I don't give a damn, Sarge. I just want to kill as many of them as possible. I want my revenge."

"It ain't about vengeance, kid. It's about freedom and restoring our rights."

"Yeah, right. And I agree. But it's also about revenge now, and you know it. You must've had somebody you love killed by now. Who was it?"

I held up my hand to say "no more." It was a question I didn't want to answer, or even think about right now. I turned away from the kid, jaw clenched. Damn him for being right.

"Okay, Sarge. I'm sorry. I'll be the lookout for awhile."

Gil settled back, took out a little stick with a small mirror on it and pushed it up over the berm top. While peering at the reflection, he commented: "Damn shame *the* big one got away, Sarge. Is it true you guys just missed him by two minutes and they used two decoy presidential helicopters?"

"Yeah," I said. "Coward left everyone behind. Then there was that wimp vice president. He slit his wrist before we could try him. You know, Gil, the guys we hung committed or authorized grievous, no - horrendous crimes. We didn't just hang them for nothing. Their worst crime, though, was trying to pull apart and destroy the goodness and greatness of this land. No forgiveness for that, and there won't be any forgiveness for us if we lose."

"Good."

"What?"

"Seriously, Sarge. You know what they say about cornered

animals and people with nothing left to lose. The most dangerous of all; definitely the most dangerous of all."

*

Barbara was strong. In many ways, stronger than me. She recovered physically and mentally from our nightmare. As she recovered, she grew angry, or should I say angrier. The personal communication line between Athenson and our committee was entirely because of Barbara's efforts.

All those new recruits were because Barb virtually demanded people on our committee go out and get someone - anyone - who either loved liberty or hated the government to join and back Athenson.

Barbara was more than a member, more than a sympathizer. Barbara was a weapon, and the government watchdogs became very aware of her. Our lives and the lives of all Athenson's backers became tense and oppressive. So it was with complete amazement that one day we found out that Barb was expecting again.

Considering the increasing mountain of problems for both us and the country, we truly weren't sure how to greet this surprising news. When we told Barbara's parents, her mother smiled and said, "It only takes a minute." Then smiled even more.

In the end, we decided it would be God's will and that life must find its own way.

"Its own way" came along a few months later. It was a boy, and we named him Samuel. We wanted him to be wise and strong.

Little Sam was a good, even necessary, distraction for the two of us for awhile. We desperately needed a break from the pressure that had built up over the last couple of years. Sam and his older sister, Rachael, although both handfuls, brought us back to real life the way it should be lived.

For a few months at least, the pressure building in our nation was eased for us, and we knew some joy and love again. It was not to last, however. Just like that: one, two, three. And ugly reality returned.

First we were informed that our private health insurance would be cancelled. Rates had already been raised substantially and benefits cut, all per government edict. Now, however, our private plan would no longer be allowed by the government, and we were being assigned a government plan with even higher rates and less coverage. On top of rising home and property taxes, this was a crushing blow.

Just in case that didn't wipe us out, the next development probably would. The government's definition of full-time work changed. You would now be considered full-time if you worked only thirty hours per week. Initially that sounded pretty good to some people. Nevertheless the truth will out, as they say. Almost everyone in a non-vital position throughout the country had their hours cut, and no extra help was hired. On top of high unemployment, those still working saw their pay decline.

All belts were tightened another notch.

The gross domestic product declined, along with a lowering of our national standard of living - again. The third slap came when the environmental agencies, at the president's urging, finally banned all coal-fired electric generation. Within sixty days it became painfully obvious how much we depended on coal for electricity and our standard of living. For awhile there was a shortage of electricity. No washing machines or air conditioners could be used on penalty of fine and arrest.

Finally things eased a bit when electric rates were allowed to rise over twenty percent. Many people, short of cash, sat in the dark at night. All this despite the fact that the coal industry had developed new scrubbers for smokestacks that took out over 98 percent of particulate pollution, and even reduced gasses by 60 percent.

As a double whammy, those fine folks in Washington next proposed banning all wood burning. Millions still burned wood to heat their homes and could afford nothing else. The environmental authorities just didn't want to hear it, so people suffered again, particularly those people in coal production or high-use areas. People there lost well over half their jobs.

Of course, everyone knew the White House was the true culprit here, but none dared speak...yet.

In light of these developments, all occurring within a month of each other, people became fired up again. When next we talked to Athenson he told us he had almost doubled the number of his volunteers, and several large contributors came forward to back him financially.

You would think good sense would prevail in this nationwide situation, and the government would recognize when they had gone too far, and back off. Not so. I had learned the painful lesson that lust for power and control feeds on itself.

*

"Lamberti. Sergeant James Lamberti."

I didn't respond initially. I was deep within my own thoughts and memories.

"Sarge!" Gil was shaking me.

"Sorry. Gil. Guess I was daydreaming again. What do you want?"

"Not me, it's that guy over there, down the line. I think he's a messenger from headquarters."

Looking to my left, I saw the messenger coming. It wasn't Paul. My heart froze. Where was Paul? Paul or not, he definitely wanted me. I waved my hand and a fed sniper took a shot at it. You know, a guy could get hurt out here.

The messenger told me I had been summoned to a conference with senior officers. Why me? I was only a sergeant. But when you're ordered, you go. Before I slunk off to command, I noticed our messenger. He was old, very old. The man had to be in his mid-eighties at least.

The Revolutionist

Oh God, have we come to this? He didn't give his name, nor did we ask it. Probably best not to get too familiar with anyone else under the circumstances.

Off we went.

Twenty minutes later, fifteen minutes of "spider walking" through mud and five minutes of sandbag alley, we arrived at headquarters. Immediately I recognized and greeted many old friends from our original campaign. Many had been promoted. They were majors and even colonels now. Many, however, were not there.

We were all guided into a great underground amphitheater and told to take seats. As soon as we sat, we heard another artillery barrage outside. It didn't last long, but it served to remind us of our real situation. As soon as it ended, a colonel somebody came out on a makeshift stage to greet us and tell us that General Ordway would be here within minutes to apprise us of the latest situation.

That's all he said, then left the stage. We glanced back and forth at each other questioningly. Were we about to be overrun, were we about to surrender, or, as someone wisecracked, were we about to declare victory?

We didn't have to wait long. General John Ordway, Supreme Commander of the Forces for Freedom; i.e., rebels, strode onto the stage, and my breath froze.

I'd first met this man over two years before. Then he was a tall, handsome, vigorous man in his mid fifties. Now I saw a tired, slightly bent, very gray man who could well have been over seventy. My heart went out to him in more ways than one.

The entire room rose to attention. At the command "as you were," we stayed on our feet and broke into applause.

It didn't matter to all of us that the man before us was clearly a beaten soul. He was our leader, one of the best leaders you could have. Every soldier in that room loved and respected him. The proof of that was the tears in the eyes of so many battle-hardened veterans.

Ordway turned to face us, sighed slightly, and hesitated a moment as his eyes swept the room.

"Ladies and gentlemen of the First Division, American Freedom Fighters." His voice was still strong, but not quite as strong as I remembered it.

"It is an honor to stand before you today, and it is I who salute you! I know well what you have suffered over the last two years, but more importantly, I know of your limitless strength and courage," Ordway declared.

"That courage is now legendary. You, yes you, will stand beside the greats; the Spartans at Thermopylae, the Revolutionary Army at Valley Forge, and the Light Brigade at Balaclava. You have accomplished miracles against an opponent of far greater numbers and far better weaponry. You have done everything asked of you and more. Regardless of how this conflict concludes, you and your comrades will live forever in the hearts, minds, and legends of the people of not only this nation, but of the whole world. God bless you."

A breathless silence swept the room.

"So why am I here? You're not fools, you know the situation is desperate. You...you are the linchpin. Although we have two more armies fighting in different parts of the country, you, the Eastern Division, is the most important. This is true because we are the closest to Washington, but even more so because of what we accomplished at the very beginning of this conflict. We... you...took Washington for several weeks, and we legally tried and convicted those who would bring our nation to ruin. The bigwigs who never got their hands dirty, but were responsible for more American deaths than any criminal gang. And as though the deaths were not enough, their true crime, their horrible crime, was robbing us of our future and our hope."

Ordway's eyes swept the room.

"They deserved worse than hanging, but it was all we could

do at the time. But such people do not accept blame for their crimes. Oh no. They cannot be wrong. Just ask them. They are always right in their own misguided, manic-driven minds. They felt our country had to be 'lowered' and 'converted,' and its people crushed to learn a lesson.

"We hoped that taking the capital and punishing many of their fanatical leaders would result in a quick end to this conflict. We hoped they would sue for peace, resign, and perhaps leave the country; and we would have let them go as long as they left this country for good. But you know what happened. Determined that their socialist ways were right, they strengthened their military with many of our new foreign arrivals, and many of their shallow, know-nothing followers, and fought back.

"With the superior weaponry at their disposal, they started winning ground again. They retook Washington, crushed one of our four armies, and have been gaining ground ever since."

General Ordway sighed, a long sigh, before he continued.

"Now, in all honesty, they have us on the ropes. This honored First Division will not be wiped out by military action, however. Oh no. They want us alive. They want to march us through the streets of Washington in chains, then hang us publicly. They want their revenge because, as always, they are the right and righteous ones."

Again, he sighed. Then he took several deep breaths, looking downward. He looked up again.

"First, and many of you have asked this many times, why are we fighting in what seems to be trench warfare? That went out well over 100 years ago. It makes us prime targets for modern weapons. Truth is, we have no choice. They've brought up massive reserves and have us completely surrounded. That berm/ trench is the only thing giving us any cover at all and we'd be wiped out without it. Yes, they could zero in on target and blow us into molecules at any time, but that's not what they want, remember? They want us alive, and, ironically, right now that's an advantage for us.

"The whole thing seems pretty hopeless, huh? Well, normally it would be, but we've uncovered some information that might give us a last chance, albeit a very desperate last chance. That, ladies and gentlemen, is why you're here. I will not reveal what that chance is right now. We'll meet here again in 24 hours for that. But I can reveal how desperate that action, if taken, will be. Look to the person on each side of you. They will not be alive in another 48 to 72 hours if we take this action. Of course, that person is also looking at you. Yes, if we take this, and succeed, we expect a casualty rate of 65 to 70 percent, and that's only if we succeed."

Ordway paused for a moment.

"I knew what I would do. After all, if we take no action we'll be marching through the streets of Washington in chains on our way to the gallows. As a soldier, as a person, I'd rather die fighting than be hung for trying to preserve our way of life and all its freedoms. Not much of a choice in my opinion, but it's not my opinion I'm after, it's yours. You are the bravest of the brave and you deserve to have your opinion heard."

"We'll do it! we'll do it!" echoed through the hall.

Ordway held up his hand to quiet them. "No, no, please. I want you to consider this for 24 hours, reach a decision, write any final letters to family and friends, and come back here tomorrow. This is the way it must be. Oh, before I forget, over the next 24 hours - in fact the next 48 hours possibly - you'll notice we are going to be fired on a lot less. There is a reason for that, and it will become clear in tomorrow's meeting.

"Ladies and gentlemen of the First Division, I salute you. You are dismissed."

The old man walked off the stage in silence.

Quickly we turned to each other. There was no decision to be made. We had all followed this man, and our political leader, Athenson, for years now. There was no turning back. Of that, we were all certain. Besides, Ordway was right again. I, too, would rather die fighting for freedom and my principles than be hung in disgrace by the slime that we fought against. After greeting and talking with a couple of old friends, plus searching for the faces of many who weren't with us anymore, I left to return to my post.

It was a curious, surreal passage. An occasional shot could still be heard in the distance, but it was much quieter than usual. There seemed an almost light or airy mode among most of my brethren as I passed.

Approaching my old friend and defender, the stump, I noticed Gil leaning back with one of the guys from the next post. I think his name was Joe. The two sat together, talking. Gil was furiously chewing on something I soon came to realize was bubble gum. It had been passed out in my absence to take our fighters' minds off the fact that rations were running dangerously low. But where had they dug up all this bubble gum? It didn't matter; we had more important things to discuss.

"Sarge, so what's the word? Do we attack tonight?" Gil was virtually jubilant.

"Not quite yet, Gil." I looked at his visitor. "Good to see you again. Joe, is it?"

"You got it right, Sergeant. So, as my buddy Gil here asked, what's the word?"

"I don't really know, guys. We're going back tomorrow for the bottom line, as it were. Tonight though, we have a decision to make." I went ahead and filled in Gil and Joe about how dangerous the general's plan would probably be. As in the assembly hall, both laughed. They said they would do whatever was required. For Division 1, there was no alternative. Every one of us had seen what was left of the bodies of our men after the government troops got through with them. Of course, that wasn't the government's official policy, but in war as in life, lots of things happen that aren't official.

Gil offered me half a ration bar, which I eagerly took. While munching, he asked me to look back into the bushes. Tom's body was gone.

"We couldn't take the smell, Sarge. It's time he was buried. Joe helped me dig a grave just behind the bushes. This lull was perfect. He...he deserved to be put to rest. It was only right."

I looked at them and slowly nodded my agreement. The last bit of ration bar stuck in my throat. I forced it down. Then something Tom once said hit me.

"You know what Tom told me about revolutions, guys? He said their true cause was passion. Oh sure, there are mean dictators, high taxes, denial of freedoms, starvation, the list goes on. But it isn't until the people get passionate about any or all of these, and more, that the dam finally bursts. It could take 100 years or it could happen in 12 hours, but once the passion hits and the hot blood rises, there's no stopping it. I told Tom he could be right. I think now, he was right. What do you guys think?"

Both just nodded their heads and muttered something low. Then, they commenced talking again and I fell back against the stump. Sure enough, the memories returned again.

Chapter Four - Ga.

It's hard to believe sometimes. The sheer number of drastic changes that took place in our country in such a short time, and bad changes to boot. No one was immune, but the middle class, the backbone of our country, was the hardest hit.

The rich were still rich, just not as rich. Though I had to acknowledge, those rich at the very top, *and* politically connected, were richer than ever. The upper middle class was hard hit, and many actually moved out of the country. Hardest hit was the central middle class and the lower middle class, almost all of whom slipped into the lower economic class.

Those in poverty saw little change, at least at first. The government still provided free housing, food, clothing, medical care, and paid all utility bills. Most of the poor actually backed all the drastic changes for awhile. They had nothing to lose at first. After a couple of years, when the allocation of food stamps was reduced and electric hours were cut, even they became irate, but it was too late.

The militarized police were now in charge of everything, and it was made clear to all that they had better toe the government line. You would think the police would back the Constitution and the people, but no. Most police backed those in power. Why? Because those in power controlled the police pension funds, and isn't that the sad bottom line? It's strange how the feeling within the country changed. There were no bright, sunny days anymore. Every day was dark and rainy despite the actual weather. It became a cancer on the soul.

I came home early one day, even from my shortened hours. Picking up the kids from our neighbor/babysitter (who had lost her long-held regular job), I proceeded to my house and started setting the table for dinner while the kids played. Suddenly, the back door slammed open. Barbara stormed in and stood there glaring at me.

"What?" I exclaimed.

At the end of a forceful sigh, she hissed, "Jim, you won't believe this! An announcement at work today; *All* health insurance policies must be exactly alike; one plan fits all. Plus, all plans must cover everything, whether you want it or not, or need it or not. It's the one-plan-fits-all policy."

Barbara took a deep breath before continuing. I was going to interrupt, but she was fuming.

"So old Mrs. Savitsky, 64 years old and a widow, MUST have birth control, prenatal and childcare coverage, while young Robert, our mail runner, is covered for female problems and birth control pills. *It's insane!* Oh, and of course, all policies will rise in price by over 35 percent, per government edict. *And* all salaries are frozen. The absolute bastards!"

She stopped talking, but continued huffing and puffing.

"Jim, what are we going to do?"

I grimaced, "Well, we could start by cutting out unnecessary things like food and electricity."

"Stop it. I'm serious." She virtually hissed.

"So am I, Barb. I just learned that we have a meeting at work tomorrow to cover pretty much the same thing."

"But...." Barb started as I held up my hand.

"I know, hon. We're both covered by your insurance, or were. Word is that all working people must carry the same insurance, even if it overlaps and is double coverage."

"That's criminal. They can't do that." Barbara stood rock solid and still even as Rachael now rushed into the kitchen to hug her mother's legs.

"Well, I guess they *are* doing it, and who's going to stop them? Big country, lots of people, big government; whether the people want it or not. You know what this required health insurance is going to do? It's going to force business to layoff full-time workers and replace them with two or three part time workers.

The Revolutionist

Less expenses all around. Many businesses will have no choice if they want to survive. Welcome to the new world."

"Oh no, *we are* going to stop them. They can't do this in a free country. Forcing you to buy something is unconstitutional!"

"Barb, Hemple died fighting town government. These are the feds we're talking about, and they've decided not to follow the constitution!"

"I don't give a damn!"

And she didn't! The first thing she did was call Athenson to tell him what she was going to do. Note: She didn't ask him what she was going to do, she told him. Athenson, being ever the wise man, approved of her plans and actions. He warned, however, of the dangers involved. Barbara didn't even respond to the warning. The game was on.

Over the next two months, Barbara planned and backed no less than a dozen large-scale demonstrations against the increasing abuse of government power. Many of these demonstrations resulted in violence and arrests. Barbara herself escaped arrest in no less than four such confrontations. She refused to back down even after two desperate calls from Athenson to be more cautious. What happened next was predictable.

*

VABOOM! The stump actually slapped up against me. A random, isolated artillery shot, sent as a reminder of power, landed not far in front of the stump. Gil, who had been napping, was startled awake and snapped his gaze toward me.

"Relax, Gil. Just a 'your friends are still here' shot."

He flashed a tired smile, leaned back, and continued napping.

*

I, too, leaned back now and searched for my interrupted memory. Ah yes, the predictable outcome of Barbara's demonstration organizing.

DeEarlon

It was just past 9 o'clock on a Tuesday night. We had just put the children to bed. I was perusing the Internet for any truthful news I could find, and Barbara had gone into the kitchen to warm a glass of wine to help her sleep. We were both startled by a sudden, hard pounding on our front door and an almost simultaneous loud but muffled shout. A moment later, the front door slammed open with a thunderous crack and armed, black-clad men rushed in.

"No one move! Those moving will be shot." Three men surrounded me, their weapons at my head. Two quickly moved to Barbara, their guns directly in her face. Almost unnoticed, her glass crashed to the floor, wine and broken shards bursting everywhere.

"What the hell?" I shouted.

"Silence!" One of the gunman in front of me put his gun barrel to my head. Barbara remained quiet.

Two men in suits nonchalantly walked through the opening that had been our front door. They looked around, then sauntered over to Barbara. They asked her to identify herself, which she did, then turned to ask me my name. I identified myself. They went on to tell us we would be accompanying them to local FBI headquarters immediately.

Before I could object, Barbara asked what would become of our children. The two men looked at each other. One finally told Barbara to call a neighbor, fast. She did, and told the neighbor to call her parents at once. The neighbors arrived within minutes, and we were whisked off to be questioned separately for three days. Three days of demanding our rights and refusing to answer any specific questions.

After three days, we were released into the custody of Attorney Joan Bleu with a warning that we would be recalled shortly for more intensive questioning. We were also informed that we would be under constant surveillance, so 'don't try anything.'

"You mean we haven't been under surveillance?" Barbara

quipped. Joan and I smiled at that, but our "hosts" only scowled.

On our way home, Joan informed us that our children were safe with Barbara's parents and that Athenson wanted to speak with us as soon as a private, untapped meeting could be arranged. We would talk about legal strategy after we got home.

Upon arriving home we called Barbara's parents first to talk to the children. Barbara then asked her parents to keep the children a bit longer just to be safe. After that we called our employers to advise them of what had happened and that we would be at work the next day.

We were both told not to bother. We had both been terminated. After hanging up, Joan informed us that the word was that virtually everyone associated with Athenson had lost their jobs because of official intimidation. She further advised us that there had been hundreds of FBI "visits" and "invitations" over the last three days. Government pressure was increasing.

*

Just as General Ordway said, it was a quieter night than usual. In fact it was nerve-rackingly boring. We did get an evening serving of rations, but whatever was in those tear-open foil packets must have been rejects from the dog pound. Despite hunger, I couldn't even eat half of it. To make matters worse, all night long we were bombarded by loud speakers asking us why we were suffering so much when just by coming over to your loving and forgiving legal government, you could start enjoying life again. Some on the line made bets as to how many of those loud speakers we could take out. We didn't take out enough.

The next morning, grumpy and tired from being awake most of the night because of those damned speakers, we actually got a halfway-decent breakfast: bread, cheese, and powdered eggs. We also got what they called coffee. Well, at least it was hot. After breakfast and before we went through the ritual of cleaning our rifles again, I asked Gil if he wanted to play cards. I'd inherited

DeEarlon

Tom Neil's deck.

Gil said, "Sure!" So we spread out a folded blanket for a table and started a rousing game of poker. In the middle of the fifth hand (Gil won the first four), word was received that we were being called in early for our decisions. That wasn't good news. We had learned long ago that anything done early was usually done out of desperation.

So in we went, keeping our heads low. Talking to my brothers on the way in, we all agreed that there was no other decision to be made. We had to follow through.

Again, entering the large, mostly underground, assembly hall, I looked for old friends. And again, I saw fewer than last time. If I could have, I would have put my hand through my chest to grip and calm my sad, throbbing heart. Blindly, I took a seat in the second row central. Glancing up and to the right, that heart I just spoke of jumped. Staring me in the face was another face that I knew well.

"Well, hello, soldier. Are you following me?"

"Jackie! Oh God, Jackie! I can't believe it's you." I had met Jackie in Washington during our occupation. Her boyfriend and she had volunteered together because they were sick of this over-zealous, controlling government. He had been killed taking the city and she then became a female Geronimo. She was actually one of the three in our unit to lead the charge into the White House. When we discovered that our traitorous president had escaped, she went wild and shot four of the guards he'd left behind. No one ever crossed Jackie.

In spite of her lingering fury after her boyfriend's death, she was actually a pleasant person to know, and a petite, golden-haired, attractive woman to boot. When I got shot through the thigh by a hidden sniper, she was the one who dressed my wound. We were all medics then. Come to think of it, we still were. Anyway, it was a very intimate procedure as the wound was, well, let's say, close to my groin.

The Revolutionist

As the weeks of our occupation rolled by, Jackie and I became very close; never intimate, but close. We shared a lot of secrets and memories. Yes, we both felt a strong sexual attraction and tension, but the closeness of our recent, personal memories stood in the way. We got separated in the almost-panicked retreat from the capital. It was a godsend to see her face and hear her voice again.

"It's me, Jim. I'm so glad to see you, and see you alive!"

"Ditto, Jack. So, where have you been? Have you been here on the line somewhere?"

"No. They chose me for a very special operation. I, well… you do what you have to, Jim. I really don't want to...."

I reached over and squeezed her hand. "Jack, you never have to explain anything to me. We all know what we have to do, or else."

She bent toward me and kissed my cheek. There was a sad, faraway look in her eyes, but a little smile on her lips. "You were always top quality, Jim. I'm so glad I know you."

I was about to reply when a voice boomed from the stage.

"Ladies and gentlemen of the First, attention!"

The entire assemblage stood as General Ordway walked onto the stage. Looking over the crowded room of nearly 600 people, he sighed.

"We all know why we're here. You have consulted your troops, and I have to ask you for the result. As stated before, this must be something that can only be asked. What I'm about to reveal can never be ordered. It is far beyond that. Remember, if we're unsuccessful, we're wiped out. But even if we're successful, up to two thirds of you will not be alive to see victory. Without further ado then, could I hear all the 'ayes' first."

The room exploded in "ayes." The old man tightened his jaw while his head trembled. "Ahhum." He cleared his throat before continuing. "Now, could I hear all the nays." Not a sound. The room was silent.

DeEarlon

The old general stood like a statue save his head and eyes slowly surveying the room. After what seemed like an eternity, he finally took a deep breath.

"I want you to know, I will be with you. I would send no one into what is about to happen unless I myself shared the risk."

Again he hesitated.

"We have information that our very esteemed president will be arriving here late tomorrow afternoon by helicopter. He will be here to see the assembled 50,000 government troops make a final assault on us. They are to capture as many of us as possible. You know why. That is why they haven't used their most modern, high-tech weapons against us. The sight of our live, torn and bleeding bodies marching through the streets on our way to mass public executions is their highest dream right now. Well, I don't intend to be marched down any street in chains by socialists, mass murderers and thieves. I will die a free man."

The assembled throng rose and exploded in shouts, hooplas, and applause.

The general continued, "There is, however, a chance, albeit a last chance, for victory here. Because of the incredible cunning, intelligence and courage of one of our own, we have that last, desperate chance. Our agent has discovered exactly where and when our traitorous president will land to observe our defeat. He wishes to gloat!"

Hisses and boos filled the room. The general held up his hand for silence. "We don't intend to let him gloat!"

Applause and hurrahs now filled the room.

"Almost beyond belief, this fool will bring with him the new vice president, and the two generals in charge of the campaign against us. Yes, they will be well protected by a 6,000-man personal body guard and the latest automated weaponry, but we have a few surprises for them too."

More cheers from the floor.

"I should mention that all this information was gathered by an

55

amazing, young female agent who is here this evening, but who wishes to remain anonymous. Anonymous or not, she deserves a standing round of applause for her selfless efforts."

The entire room stood and clapped. I rose slapping my hands together wildly. Looking down, I saw Jackie still sitting, her eyes cast down.

"Jackie, come on. Clap for our agent," I cried. Slowly she rose, her hands coming together weakly in mild approval. As I looked at her, the truth occurred to me. Jackie returned my gaze, quickly holding a finger to her lips. My claps slowed, but I did not speak.

Ordway continued.

"Thanks to her information, we have devised our own plan to penetrate the traitorous dogs, shield and capture them. They are the black heart of our nation's betrayal and virtually the entire brain trust of that betrayal. Without them, well, when you cut off the head of the snake, you know what happens. This is an all-or-nothing effort. I have detailed plans for each of you.

"We will form into completely different units, some with most unusual orders. Those orders will be passed out when I leave the stage. Our objective is twofold. One, to capture these criminals alive and reverse strategy on them. Failing that, to kill them, quite bluntly, so that their army and its campaign will be thrown into chaos. Our Second Division, in the Midwest, is part of the plan. I expect, as already stated, that even if we succeed, there won't be enough of us left to be an effective fighting force."

He fell silent a moment to take several deep breaths.

"This may be the last time I see any of you, or you me. As always, I know you will serve above and beyond." He looked down and sighed. Then, lifting his head high and fast, said, "May God be with you. May God be with all of us." He walked from the stage with thunderous applause as his minions rushed out with hundreds of sealed folders. They held up unit numbers for each separate leader to come forward for orders and the combined plan.

DeEarlon

I hesitated. Standing beside Jackie, our eyes slowly came up to meet.

"Jackie, I....."

"Jim, please. Don't ask. I did what had to be done. I hate them. I hate them so completely.... I have to go now. The job isn't over. We...probably won't meet again, Jim. You know, if things had been different; if we hadn't had others to think about, things might have been different."

She broke off quickly, reached up to kiss me, this time on the lips. She squeezed my hands and rushed off into the crowd. I stood, silent and shaken. How many times can you lose someone you love? Damn!

"Lamberti, Lamberti! Hey, get your butt over here and pick up your orders. You gotta talk to two other unit leaders before you leave here."

The talks with the other unit leaders lasted almost an hour. With them was Colonel Derman, the rebels' top expert on covert operations. Colonel Derman had been the government's top expert, but couldn't stomach the nation's new direction or its new leaders. When hostilities began, he switched sides fast.

Plans had to be memorized then and there, then burned in a large barrel on one side of the hall. Gil and I, plus the other two units, would be the point of the spear. All three units contained 'survivors': soldiers who just seemed to have the knack of living through anything, and that's exactly what was important here. While the vast majority made a massive, hard penetration of government forces to open the way to the presidential helicopter, my company would covertly approach and try to capture, or if necessary kill, those on the chopper. It was made clear that the plan had little if any chance of succeeding. If it could be done, however, the rebels would hold the winning hand.

Some questioned the plan, pointing out the very small chance of success. But further, one unit leader asked if others wouldn't just take over government leadership. Then the secret was dropped. Yes they would, Colonel Derman said, but the only others who could do this were now on the West Coast, completely surrounded by our Third Army. They had not received the kind of protection the president, vice president, and two top generals on the chopper received, because no one seriously thought they could lose.

That second string on the West Coast would be an easy capture or kill. The elimination of the these two groups would leave only a small cadre of, as General Ordway said many times, complete idiots in charge. Checkmate…or so we hoped.

Meeting, timing, positioning were the last things we discussed before breaking up. We were told before we actually moved out to implement said plan, extra ammunition, grenades, and a special weapon would be delivered to our current positions. Be prepared.

Returning to "stump one" a few minutes later, I started going over all the intricacies of this last, desperate plan. As overwhelmingly important as this was, though, I couldn't keep my mind from drifting back over my life and loves. There was my wife, Barbara...my wife, my life, loved forever; my kids, Rachael and Sam; and finally Jackie. What can I say? The heart is fickle and complicated, just like life and this plan.

Chapter Five - Conn.

Gil was talking to someone. As I got closer, I could see it was a black soldier with a green bandana tied tightly around his head, pirate style.

"Hey, Sarge, this is Corporal Marv Taylor. He's from the squad, ahh, a couple of squads down from us. He's bored as hell and just visiting."

I extended my hand. "Nice to meet you, Corporal. How are you and your squad doing? Let's see, that's Bill Dupre's squad, right?"

Taylor looked down, then up. "Was... until yesterday morning. Bill took a piece of shrapnel through the throat. Bled out before we could stop it. That's my squad now, Sarge, if that's what you can call it. Only got three men left besides me."

"Sorry, Taylor. For you and for Bill. We're really getting down there in numbers, aren't we?"

The corporal sighed, "Yeah, this section of the line is gettin' pretty damn thin. If we get hit with any strength...." He trailed off.

My inner thoughts went to how few men were left in this army. Did they really have enough personnel to mount a major wedging attack against the government forces? I wasn't supposed to tell the corporal about any of the "big plan." It wasn't his squad. On the other hand, if Bill was dead....

"Corporal, were you or Bill called into headquarters in the last 24 hours?"

"Well," Taylor started, "since Bill was dead, he didn't go anywhere, and I sure as hell got no invitation."

I thought a moment before deciding. "Well Marv, I guess it falls on me to give you the word. I hope this isn't happening all over this man's army. Damn poor communications. Okay, by tonight you and all the units around us will get special orders to unite into a large company. The commander of that company will be named in the communique you will get. There will be a hard press on the government forces. Exactly when and where will be in the communique."

"About time we did something. I'm tired of just sitting here and getting picked off." Taylor reflected a moment. "Ya know, we can't win. They'll crush us. Not that I care. We all knew it was only a matter of time for us anyway." He looked up. "Be an honor to move out with you, Sergeant. You are something of a legend, you know."

A slow smirk appeared on my face.

"Some legend. Anyway, we won't be moving out with you, Corporal." His gaze fell on Gil. "This young man and I have another assignment."

Again I hesitated. "Corporal Taylor, you called it right. There won't be many of us coming through this thing. You should have had the question presented to you already as to whether you wished to participate in this action. They did give us a choice. It is, as you point out, a virtual suicide assignment. But on the other hand...."

"You know damn well, Sergeant, there is no 'other hand.' We either die fighting or those bastards will kill us anyway. I'm in."

I hunkered down and extended my hand again. Taylor and I shook. "A pleasure to serve with you, Corporal."

"A pleasure to serve with you, Sergeant."

Corporal Marvin Taylor rose. "Well, guess I should return to my squad and present the news to them. I wonder what they'll vote - to go or stay?" He laughed as he turned and began to walk. After a few steps, they heard him call back, "See you in hell, gentlemen."

Gil and I both waved, then settled back silently. After a few minutes, Gil asked, "Hey, Sarge, you know what Marv told me?"

"That he had a winning lottery ticket and the government won't let him collect."

"Ha ha! Very funny! No, that both his younger brother and sister are somewhere in the government forces. That's weird, huh?"

"Not really, Gil. That's why they said the Civil War was 'brother against brother.' It happens a lot in a civil war."

"Civil war? I thought this was a rebellion. Which is it, a civil war or a rebellion?"

"A little bit of both, I guess, Gil; and a lot of pure hellfire."

A light artillery barrage opened up from the government side, with shells whizzing high over their heads and exploding harmlessly far beyond rebel lines.

"Sarge, it's just like you said Ordway told you. They're reminding us they're there, but they really don't want to hit us just yet."

"Yeah, I hope it all goes like he said, kid." I leaned back and my bloodshot eyes grew heavy.

*

"Wimps, that's what we've all become - wimps!" One of the older members of the local Conservative Party Town Committee held the floor. They were having an impromptu meeting of the most conservative members, and they didn't want their statements on record.

"Mr. Jepsen, please lower your voice and give someone else a chance to speak. This is, after all…."

"Ah, to hell with the lot of you! If this was back in my day, we'd just grab our guns and head for Washington." Mr. Jepsen was shaking his right fist in the air now.

"Absolutely, and you'd all be mowed down by automatic weapons fire and tanks before you reached Pennsylvania Avenue," John Barret shouted from his seat.

"Ah, you're all a bunch of…. I can't say it because there's ladies present." Jepsen sat down, still fuming.

"I don't see any ladies," Barbara uttered in a loud, mock

whisper. The assemblage giggled.

I rose. "Okay, look. We have a very serious situation here. Our central government is out of control and on a dangerous power trip. They're trampling on our rights and even those of our own party in Washington refuse to stand up for us, the average citizen. We have to find a way to retain, no, to *regain* our rights. As you know, they've already taken virtual control of the Internet and placed taxes on it. They have...."

"They're making fools of us around the world," a neatly dressed, middle-aged lady, relatively new to the committee, spoke up. "Terrible international decisions are coming out of Washington, and all the major countries are laughing at us behind our backs."

From the back of the room another voice rose from an unidentified person. "Did you hear what they plan next? They plan to confiscate our private retirement plans and replace them with a sort of second social security plan completely controlled by them, and they'll tax it just like regular income. *They are thieves!*"

A low rumble of agreement swept the room.

"Well, we know they're thieves. That's one of the reasons we're here!" John Barret spoke up.

"What do we do about it?" The sentiment echoed from everywhere in the room.

"That's a very good question." All eyes looked up as two new figures entered the room. An invitation had been left for Attorney Joan Bleu to this impromptu meeting earlier in the day. Busy with other appointments, she had finally arrived, and she had brought a guest with her, Professor Athenson.

"I wish I could give you a definitive answer to that question," Athenson said as he and Joan strode to the front and took two empty seats.

Barbara, the true *de facto* leader, rose. "Professor Athenson, it's an honor that you and Attorney Bleu could make it.

Considering the question, could we call upon you two to give us your opinions?"

Athenson and Bleu conferred quietly for a few seconds, then Athenson rose to face the assembled members.

"I hate to use a cliche, but it fits so well: Our nation has become a 'boiling cauldron.' We face so many problems, and our political leaders are *not* solving them. In fact, they are precipitating most of them. They do this to gain pure power, as has happened in so many other nations. I fear they not only will not stop, but will, in fact, increase their dark momentum. No amount of reason or humanity will avert them from their course. To make the situation even worse, many uneducated or under-educated people support them, believing this is the true role of government; that is, making our decisions for us.

"Take, for instance, the wonderful new direction they are taking us in. If you've been paying attention, you know they have announced plans to make us into a cashless society. This is being presented as a remarkable new benefit for us as a truly advanced society. They plan to issue a government debit card to everyone. Where there is no cash, there will be no robberies or muggings, so they say. There is a complete omission of the fact that a government debit card means the end of all privacy forever. The feds will be able to review every single thing you do down to buying a stick of gum. It also means the end of freedom. If they don't like what you're doing or who you're supporting, your card can be suddenly overdrawn or even cancelled. Those silly old bank notes or, better yet, gold and silver coins, represent true freedom and independence. Oh, and as for the safety angle of no cash? That's absurd. A thief can steal your card and wipe you out in a few hours. That card will represent absolute, complete control of your life and everything around it."

Athenson paused for a moment.

"Of course, we know that a republican democracy cannot survive under such control and horrendous leadership for long.

The Revolutionist

"So what *can* we do? We can't count on the vote. We find far too many of our citizens willing to accept this atrocity. They are all too willing to be told what to do, where to live, what to eat, where and even if they can go to a doctor. I could go on. They are told to strip the rich of all they have to give to the those who don't have, not realizing that they only make those in government richer while driving out the movers and shakers that make the country rich. Even if we could, in fact, win a vote, those numbers would be 'magically changed' by the time they were legally recorded. Such is the sorry state of our beloved country today.

"Again then, what can we do? Since the possibility of winning an honest vote has tragically disappeared, it leaves us with few options other than force: force of arms."

"Oh God, no! Do you know what you're saying?" a young woman shouted from the audience.

"Indeed I do, young lady, and I quake at saying it myself. When I was young, I never would have believed such a thing was necessary, but look at the condition of our country, and our freedoms within that country. Our rights and freedoms disappear almost daily, as does our standard of living. The people of this nation, only 50 or 60 years ago, would never have stood for our leaders doing the things they're doing now, but today, the people sit placidly by while being crushed. I do not enjoy saying these things. What I enjoyed was the older, freer America, but that is not the reality of today. We have been robbed of that wonderful land." The young woman convulsed in sobs. "If anyone has any better ideas, I'm sure we would all like to hear them." Athenson raised his open hands wide into the air, questioningly.

"I do," an unknown voice echoed.

Chapter Six - Mass.

I don't know what woke me but, glancing to my right, I saw Gil dozing. All around him the air was still and quiet. Nothing moved. I checked my watch, and my heart leapt. I was long overdue back at headquarters for final answers and preparations. I jumped into the air, quickly thought about what I did, and collapsed back down onto my knees, my heart still pounding madly. I was lucky not to have been shot by a sniper. Falling forward, I started to spider crawl back along the path to headquarters. Moving beyond all deliberate speed, I cut the palm of my hand and tore a hole in a knee of my trousers. Reaching the tunnel opening, I stood and actually ran the last couple hundred yards.

"I'll be damned," one of the sentries at the main door quipped. "You ain't dead after all."

I just stared at him and continued on to the front of the hall where several large groups were assembled. I saw a waving hand go up from a person in one group. Assuming they were waving at me, I walked toward that group.

"Sergeant Lamberti, we were about to give up on you. Sergeant Jacobs here was about to go out looking for you. Is there any acceptable reason you are so late? Technically, Sergeant, we could charge you...."

"No! Ah, no, sir; I have no acceptable excuse. And I'm sorry for interrupting you, sir. I could lie, but I won't."

Colonel Derman stared at him a moment. "Your record is so outstanding, Sergeant, I'm going to give you a pass on this. I'm going to assume there was more than sufficient reason for your tardiness. I'm going to further assume you understand the critical importance of what we are about to do, and that you are still in shape to do it. Am I correct, Sergeant?"

"You are, sir." I saluted the colonel.

Colonel Derman looked me up and down with tightly narrowed

eyes. "Damn man, you're more of a mess than usual!"

Then he slapped me on the back and led me toward the group. On the way, Derman noticed a peculiar scar under my left ear. It was in the shape of a Y.

"How did you get that scar, Sergeant?"

"Oh, got that when I was a kid, sir. Bunch of boys messing around. One of them smacked me with end of a metal rod. aven't thought of it in years, Colonel."

"As long as you don't claim it as a war injury in the future, Sergeant." We both laughed as we reached the group.

"Alright, ladies and gentlemen, we will begin again. The reason we wanted you here so much, Sergeant Lamberti, is to congratulate you. You are 'Project Victory's' leader."

Now I listened intently. Maps were pored over and timetables disclosed. Several special weapons were passed out. I had seen one of these specials before and was throughly awed by it. I knew how special it was. If the rebels only had a few thousand of these, there might well be no question of their victory.

The meeting of the whole group lasted almost an hour. At that point, most were dismissed. I was detained for special instruction. In exactly an hour and a half after I left here, all of the special operations group would meet back at the location, stump central, for complete and final instructions. There the whole group would await the beginning of Project Victory.

Colonel Derman gripped my hand. "You know the odds Sergeant, but you also know...."

"Yes, sir. Well aware of the odds, sir." I squeezed the colonel's hand tightly.

"We'll all be there, you know. Every one of us participates in this. Every one of us will be needed, but you and your men are the linchpin. God be with you, sergeant...you and yours."

We saluted and broke off. I picked up the special armament for myself and Gil, and started back, a little slower this time. With the extra burden of the added weapons and ammunition,

I couldn't spider walk, so I crouched as much as possible. I noticed rations were being passed out, much larger rations than usual. No explanation necessary there.

As I walked, my thoughts ran deep. This could well be the last ordinary walk of my life. Could this be my last day on Earth? What had my life counted for? Had there been purpose here, and more to the point, had that purpose been accomplished? Yes, these thoughts had occurred before, but I've never had the luxury of so certain an end, or so much time to ponder.

Then my mind and heart reached out to Rachael and Sam. Oh God, hopefully my in-laws got them into Canada. Would their lives be good? Would they ever think of or know about their father? And did that matter, as long as they had decent, happy lives? Tears now flooded my eyes and poured down my cheeks. I hadn't seen my children in over two and a half years. They must have grown so much. I clenched my jaw tightly.

Barbara. Would I ever see Barbara again? Lifting my eyes, I muttered, "See you soon, lover. I do love you, you know, and always have. Don't be mad at me for Jackie. Nothing happened there. As for what might have been with her if things had continued…. Hey, I'm still flesh and blood down here. It's been a long time since…you know. I still love you, always."

I blew a kiss skyward, stopped and wiped the tears from my eyes, and took a deep breath. I muttered to myself, "Hey buddy, you've still got a job to do. Let's get on with it. You don't know what's going to happen, but you do know that other lives depend on you. *Let's go, you slacker!*"

Ten more minutes and I was back at stump central. Gil pushed a loaded ration tray toward me, smiling. As for Gil himself, he was smoking.

"When they came around with the chow, they asked us if we were smokers. I said yes and they gave me six cigarettes. This is my second and I saved three for you."

Gil handed over three cigarettes, all slightly bent. "Sorry about that, Sarge." I just smiled.

As I was in the middle of my much-larger-than-usual ration tray, the loud speakers started from the government side. They blasted out the usual crap of "Surrender and you'll be pardoned."

Ha! They'd discussed this earlier at headquarters. I suddenly felt numb, and swallowed the last of my meal mechanically. It was the beginning move on the chess board. One way or the other, this was the last campaign: checkmate soon - very soon.

*

"I repeat. I do!" The stranger now stood and swept his gaze around the room. He was tall and thin, with a narrow, mealy face and dark, short hair. Where had I seen him before? Suddenly, I recognized him. He was the one who'd run from my grip at a past meeting: the government spy. He'd said his name was Mike Paine, but I'm sure that was just an alias.

"Who are you and how did you get in here?" someone shouted.

"You'll all find out." The stranger held up an open palm. "You know, you're all playing a dangerous game here. Challenging the government can be very bad for your well being. It's much better for all of you to let the big things be handled by professionals in government, while the average citizen just sits back and enjoys life. Life is good here. This is the greatest country in the world."

"It used to be!" Barbara was on her feet now, staring at the interloper. "People like you are destroying it. I recognize you. You're that spy from the government. My husband said your name was Mike…ah, yes, Paine. How appropriate is that, huh?"

Barb now scanned the faces in the room and got murmuring agreement. "You are a 'pain,' sir and so is your government. People in this country should expect little, if any, interference in their lives from honest government. Instead we get interference in *everything*! We're being told what we can do and even how to do it. Plus we're being taxed out of all we have for the privilege of being bossed around. In effect, being charged for the establishment of dictatorial socialism. How dare you even show your face here!"

Loud murmurs and "here heres" filled the room.

The government man was laughing now. "You people are all fools. Clinging to those silly, archaic beliefs in freedom. This is a modern world, folks. Get used to it. Big countries, fast times, modern world, they all require *big* government. The government makes the decisions and you do as you're told. You'll have a roof over your head and food in your belly. Don't expect any more. But one thing you can expect: Get out of line and you'll lose the roof and the food.

"Look, the people in Washington are being as gentle with you 'citizens' as possible. They're moving slowly so you aren't too shocked with the transition to a modern world."

"Modern? You mean the way it was in the old Soviet empire?" Barbara shot back. "They didn't like it much when it started, and they sure as hell didn't like it in the end, with how many countries rising up to throw off that socialist crap?"

Barbara was truly cranked up now. She was seething.

Mike Paine's face, if that truly was his name, was drawn up in a sadistic smile. He snickered as he talked. "You'll learn. You'll all learn. The time of individual freedom and meaningful elections is over. Government is just too big today. The issues are too big. People have to learn to let government run things. That's the way it is. That's their job; and you *will* learn."

Mr. Paine was still snickering as one of the men sitting close to him rose and punched him squarely in the face. He fell backward, tumbled over his seat and onto the floor behind him. In a flash, two other unidentified men, who had been standing in the back, rushed forward to seize the man who had thrown the punch.

Then the room exploded. Virtually every person, man and woman, descended on the two men, and it became a brawl for all. The chaos continued with screams and the sound of cracking, crashing furniture from every corner of the room, until two thunderous booms froze everyone.

"*Freeze!* The next person to move gets shot!" Mike Paine stood behind the entangled mob of humanity, gun in hand. Blood from his nose trickled down his lips and chin. He had fired two shots into the ceiling.

"Everybody stand aside. Larry, Drew, get back here with me." The two agents stood, disentangled themselves, and stumbled back beside Paine.

"The deal is this: I could take you all into custody and you'd never be heard from again. But that's not what I'm going to do. As I said, you will learn. There will be some big changes in your community folks, and you won't like them. As for you, Mr. Athenson, expect a visit from some of my colleagues soon. I'd have my affairs in order if I were you, sir."

Paine looked from person to person, finally setting his gaze on the man who had punched him. "I don't know who you are, sir, but I will soon. I'm not going to charge you with anything now, but I have your picture and any time you get out of line again…. Do I make myself clear?"

The man just stood there, motionless.

"Further," his eyes continued to sweep, finding Barbara. "We already know who you are, lady. Any more flap from you, anywhere: same thing, you disappear."

They turned to leave. As they reached the door, I spoke up. "Did it ever occur to you, and your kind, that *you* might disappear, Mr. Paine?"

Again, Paine stopped and turned. "Damn, you jerks are dumb. You're going down! You can't beat the government, you idiots! We're a mountain, and you're just some tiny bump to be run over." He turned to leave.

"We are no bump, Mr. Paine." I still stood, glaring at the government agent. "In fact, we're less than that. We are dirt, sand, and pebbles all driven by a passionate wind, and eventually, Mr. Paine, we will wear that mountain down."

DeEarlon

Paine, his body already half turned toward the door, curled his lips viciously and snickered. Then he and his compatriots finished their turn and disappeared through the door.

All was silent for a few seconds, then John Barret spoke. "Oh boy, we're in for it now."

A single, ragged voice arose from the crowd, "Dissent, opposition: They've both become crimes. The government has criminalized opposition!"

"Didn't we always know this would happen?" Athenson stepped forward. "From the moment this bunch got into power, we could see what they were up to. Now, we're backed into the proverbial corner. We have only one way to go."

"The problem is, professor," Attorney Joan Bleu chimed in, "they know that, too."

Chapter Seven - Md.

"Who put you in charge?" Pete Kenburg, leader of another surviving unit, asked. "We survived as much crap as you two did. Why can't I be in charge?" Pete not only appeared a little upset about me being the leader, but he was a bit wobbly too.

"Hey!" Gil jumped up.

"It's alright, Gil. I'll handle this." I was cool and calm. I'd also smelled Pete's breath and wondered where he got the booze. I passed over that question at the moment.

"Look, guys, I didn't appoint me, Central Command did. I can only assume they had a good reason to do so. If you don't like it, go talk to them."

"It's okay with me, Jim." Sergeant Mark Ferran, leader of the third group, piped up. He flipped his head toward Kenburg and smiled.

"And me too," Corporal Sanchez, Kenburg's underling, spoke as he suddenly kicked Kenburg hard in the crotch, causing him to ball up with a guttural shriek. "I put up with this jerk long enough. Too long! I don't know how he survived so long. He's always comin' up with some hooch from somewhere. He shouldn't be alive. Billy, another guy we had, saved this ass's life once and lost his in the process. I wish Billy was here. Billy was a good man."

"You bastard!" Kenburg lunged at Sanchez, pulling his field knife at the same time. The butt of Gil's rifle stopped Kenburg flat as it met his skull. He lay there on the ground, a small trickle of blood making its way through his hair.

I sighed, "Oh damn. Now what?"

"I'm sorry, guys." Sanchez just stared at Kenburg. "He wouldn't have been any good anyway. He was drunk, and he wasn't any good when he was sober. We always covered for him."

DeEarlon

"Well, he's still alive." I removed my hand from Kenburg's neck. "But if he ever wakes up, it'll be long after this thing is over." I looked up at the rest of the assembled group. "What do you think, guys? Can we do this with just the five of us?" Each now looked back and forth.

"What do you think, Gus? We haven't heard a word from you." Sergeant Ferran addressed the rest of his unit, which consisted of one man, Gus. It was Gus; just Gus, no last name, no rank.

"We can do it." Gus' lips barely moved as the dry words poured out. He could move though, like the devil himself, it was said, when he had to.

"Okay guys, we go." I nodded at each of them. "We've gone over the plan, such as it is. When the entire First moves out, we stay behind until the enemy is fully engaged. They'll try to draw the government troops into two separate actions on each side of us, or at least as much as they can. We then try to quietly slip up through the action toward an open field about a mile and a half in front of us. In that field, if all goes as planned, a large chopper will be landing with the president, vice president, secretary of defense, and their two top generals. They will be backed up by at least twelve top bodyguards. They are so confident of final victory they want to be here to see it, gloat, and be filmed inspecting the defeated rebels.

"I know it's a desperate plan, but it's all we've got left. Remember, we try to capture them if we can. Captives are better than bodies. It's the old 'remove the top of the pyramid and the whole structure falls apart' plan. Any questions?"

"Yeah." Sanchez was smiling. "Is God gonna' back us on this one or not? Cuz' I gotta tell ya', without Him...well, ya know."

"And we got a choice, Sanchez?" Gil put his two cents in.

"Oh, I didn't say that. I know we got no choice. I'm in regardless. I'm just sayin' we better start prayin'." Sanchez leaned back and shut up.

I looked around the group, one at a time. "Okay guys, clean

your weapons, write your final letters, clear your minds. We have only hours left." I settled back.

Most soldiers are quiet and introspective before big battles. Suppressing the fear, they think of other things, like what have you done with your life. I was no exception, but I had done this a thousand times before at the beginning of a thousand battles, or so it seemed. This time, forcing my mind in another direction, I started looking up and down the line at the various and sundry people who had stepped forward to risk everything for that most elusive, yet alluring, concept: freedom. I was always amazed at the mixture of those who had stepped up. To my right was Marvin Taylor, a black man, and with Marvin was a milky white, red-headed kid named Hendrixson. The two others with them were sort of light tan. I didn't know their names or heritage.

To my left was a very tall guy named Lukko. Estonian or something, I thought. Lukko's energetic corporal was an Indian guy, couldn't remember his name right now, but he was mad as hell that he'd come to this country for more opportunity, and found it and freedom dying.

Right here at stump central, look at our mix. There is Sanchez, Hispanic. I'd run into thousands of Hispanics who had joined the rebel cause. And yes, he'd been surprised. After all, when so many had first come here, they'd been largely dependent on the government for survival initially. One would think they'd be loyal to the big, central government. As I thought about it, however, I finally realized that they came here to escape grinding poverty and the overreaching, complete big government control that had caused it. Most had no desire to repeat this fiasco or live under it again.

There is, or was, Tom Neil, my dead buddy. Tom was a fourth generation American of Irish heritage. The key there, according to Tom himself, was *Irish*! No one was going to tell an Irishman how to live. Period. I smiled gently and partially turned my head back toward Tom's grave.

DeEarlon

Oh yes, and Gil, the remainder of my present unit. Gil was part Italian and French heritage, but 100 percent Anglo. He kept telling me about constitutional rights and even mentioned the Magna Carta once. It doesn't get any more Anglo than that.

I glanced skyward. "And you, lover. Let's see, you were part German and Scots, I believe." I blew a kiss toward the darkening clouds. My head then fell downward for a minute, finally snapping upward.

Then there was me. Well, I've got an Italian name, but my father was also part Polish. Mom, she had ten or twelve different nationalities in her, including, so she claimed, Native American. I think she said Seneca. When she got mad at some big-government move, she would say that no one was going to take this country away from us again. I snickered. Mom and Barbara both had tempers.

Wandering up and down the line again, in my mind at least, I saw all the different "rebels." Different colors, heritages, religions, accents; different, different, different. All brought together and putting their lives on the line for that magic, yet indefinable concept: freedom.

It is indefinable. It doesn't mean you can do just anything; there are limits, but it does mean you can run your own life without government interference. As long as you directly hurt no one else, they must leave you alone, even if you make bad and foolish personal decisions. Governments always, eventually, go too far, though. They begin to believe *they* are the nation, not the people. That's when the trouble - the commands - begin.

That's when the magic should begin; the magic of freedom. Is the magic of freedom enough to hold these people together and is it strong enough to win this fight? As my eyes swept along the line, it didn't seem so right now. That monstrous juggernaut just across the killing field is crushing us. That has happened so many times before in the world.

I know, I know. We all thought it would be different this time.

The Revolutionist

It wasn't.

Each one of us on this side had his or her own reason for being here, but every one of us finally just got tired of government control. There was more government control, and more, and more, and.... It was endless. Along with our lowered standard of living and the curtailment of our long-accepted rights, people got mad; really mad. Then there was the fear, a low, shadowy fear of big, growing government that grew every day.

One day, it just snapped.

*

"Mommy, I'm hungry." Rachael had just come in from the school bus, dropped her school bag, and stood sad-eyed in front of her mother.

Barbara looked down with care and sympathy at her older child. "Did you do a lot of running around today, baby?"

"No. They wouldn't let us eat."

"What?" Barbara thought a minute, then smiled. "Did you lose your lunch bag, young lady?"

"No, mommy!" Rachael was firm in a shy, childish manner. "Our principal, Miss Ducbak, visited our room and told us we couldn't eat what we brought from home unless it was on a list she gave us. The list is in my lunch bag. She told us even the stuff in the cafeteria will be only what the government allows us to eat. Everything else, she said, is bad for us."

Barbara started to speak, but was struck silent. She reached into her daughter's book sack, pulled out the lunch bag, and opened it. The salami sandwich and fresh plum were still inside, untouched. There was an additional item however: a folded note.

The note was from the school district's central office and was signed by the superintendent of schools. It pointed out that, on account of new federal regulations, which the district soundly endorsed, all student lunches must comply with new federal guidelines. It pointed out that, among many other foods, cold meat sandwiches and stone fruits would no longer be allowed for students in the district. Cold meats, especially with mayonnaise, were very unhealthful for anyone, particularly children. As for stone fruits, there was a true, though slim, danger of choking, so they, too, were banned from now on.

Two following pages listed the only acceptable foods for students henceforth; on threat of student expulsion and parental fines. Barbara crumpled the papers in her hand and began to breathe hard. She suddenly took note of the fact that Sam wasn't there.

"Rachael, where's Sam?"

"While you were reading, Mommy, he ran right past you and into the kitchen. They wouldn't let him eat either."

Barbara took a deep breath, held it a second, then ran to find her phone. All school district phone lines were busy. She called a friend, another parent with children in the same school. Her friend said her children had gone through the same indignity, and, no, her friend couldn't get a call through to the school either, or the superintendent's office. Both agreed to meet later at the school after contacting other parents, lots of parents.

As I walked through the door, Barbara rushed up and quickly explained what had happened with the children at school that day. She asked me to stay with Rachael and Sam while she met with at least three dozen other angry parents at school to complain about these sudden changes and their children going hungry.

I reminded her of the "guidelines" for school lunches that had been sent home before. She replied, "Exactly! Guidelines, not *government commands!*" And off she went.

At the time, we were all angry, but we had no idea what this night would bring.

I remember sitting there, watching some mystery thriller on TV. The children had been tucked into bed. It was well past 10 p.m. and I was beginning to worry about Barbara. Reaching over for the phone, I was about to call her when I saw headlights flash across the living room windows. Her car, I assumed, had just pulled into the driveway. Replacing the phone, I leaned back to await my wife's arrival through the side door. That didn't happen. There was a sudden pounding on the front door. Confused and worried, I virtually jumped to the door and quickly peered out cautiously before actually opening it. The people outside were the first parents Barbara had called. The handle was almost torn off as I yanked the door open.

"Margaret, Ben, what's wrong? Where's Barbara?"

"Jim, I don't know how to tell you this." Our friend Margaret was stammering.

"Jim, Barb was arrested or almost arrested." Ben was a bit more direct.

"Arrested? Arrested for what?" As I finished the question, a police car pulled up. Ben and Margaret glanced back toward the cruiser.

"There was," Ben stared wide-eyed at me now, "a kind of fracas. Oh, hell, there was a riot. Barb was able to get hold of your friend Athenson, the professor. There must have been a hundred or more parents outside the school." Ben was talking fast now as two policemen approached us. "They wouldn't let us in; we demanded in, and the police were called. Athenson started to make a speech and a cop grabbed him. Some other lady slugged the cop. Another cop tackled her, and her husband, I guess, tackled the cop. Then all hell broke loose!"

"Mr. Lamberti? Are you James Lamberti?" The law had arrived.

"I am. What in God's name is going on here?" I stepped out and toward the two officers.

"Please keep your distance, sir. We don't want any trouble."

"I don't want any trouble either. I just want to know what happened to my wife."

"That's what we'd like to know also, sir. Is she here?" asked the other officer.

"Does it look like she's here? I'd like...." I began.

"Please don't smart mouth us, sir! We are looking for Barbara Lamberti. We have a warrant for her arrest!"

"*For what?*" I screamed back.

"Inciting to riot and assault."

"*Barbara?*" My jaw dropped open.

"Is she here, sir?" One of the cops asked again. "Because this could be considered hot pursuit, we don't need a warrant to search your house. If you resist or attempt to block us, you will be placed under arrest."

"I...ah." Now I was stammering. "*No*, she isn't here! I was waiting for her to come home. I thought it was her when Marge and Ben pulled in."

One of the cops then cocked his head toward our two friends. "Yeah, about you two. You were present at the riot, weren't you?"

Marge stepped back silently while Ben nervously replied. "We were there; I mean, we saw it, but we weren't part of it."

The two policemen looked at each other for a moment with no comment. Then one said that, since they had no warrant for them, they could go, but they wanted to see positive ID's and they would be called in later for statements. They could leave now!

Ben and Margaret slowly departed. As they reached their car, one policeman raced over to it, demanding to search it. Finding nothing, they were allowed to go.

Now they turned their full attention to me. "Shall we go in, sir?"

I backed into the house, the police directly following. They searched the house thoroughly, with my permission, of course, as they kept pointing out. I warned them about Rachael and Sam sleeping. In truth, they were quiet and respectful. The children never woke, and that at least, was something. But in the back of my mind, the worry about my wife was growing.

After 15 or 20 minutes, the police left, with a strong admonition to contact them as soon as my wife contacted me in any way. Assuring them I would, they left. Of course I knew they'd be watching the house and almost certainly tapping our phone line. How, in God's name, would Barbara get in touch with me. More importantly, was she safe? It was going to be a long night. I went into the kitchen and made a large pot of coffee. Sleep would not come this night.

Thud. What was that? Oh, I'd dozed off for a few minutes. Checking the clock, it was 6:45 in the morning. With enormous effort, the sofa and me parted company. I rose to greet the new day. No Barbara yet. What was that noise? Oh, the cat had jumped down from something. Heading back into the kitchen, I poured a stale cup of cold coffee and stuck it in the microwave. Then, I remembered the kids. It was already late.

Going to each door, with some vigorous knocks, the children were awakened and told to get ready for school quickly. At a very hurried breakfast, Rachael asked where mom was. What can you tell your child about her missing mother?

"Honey, Mom is sleeping late. It was a long meeting last night."

"I'll bet Mom really gave it to them, right Dad?" Rachael was grinning broadly.

"Oh yes, honey, she really did." I took some money out of my wallet, dividing it between Rachael and Sam. "You guys will have to buy lunch today. There's no time to make it."

Sam piped up, "I don't like what they have, Daddy. That's why Mom makes it."

"Yeah, I don't like it either," Rachael's face twisted.

Looking at them both for a moment, I said, "I don't like *anything* they're serving in the public schools today guys."

Rachael continued, "You know what our teacher told us a few days ago, Daddy? She said we have an obligation to be loyal to our government over our families. And, we have to serve the public good over anything we do for ourselves. What does that mean, Daddy?"

What do you say to your children when they're fed this socialist gibberish? With Barbara on the back of my mind and with time being late, I copped out.

"I'll explain it later, kids. It's late and you've missed the bus. Grab your book bags and let's go."

On the way to school, I noticed a large, dark car behind us all the way. It did not follow me back home.

Within half an hour of returning home, I placed a call to the police, hoping for any information about Barbara; no help, only another warning to contact them if Barbara contacted me. I also placed calls to Professor Athenson's office and to another couple I knew had attended the meeting the previous night. No one answered at either place. I left messages. While about to place a call to Barbara's parents, the phone rang. It was Joan Bleu, the attorney.

"Hi Jim, it's so good to talk to you again." Her voice and demeanor were bright, cheerful and light-hearted. "You know, me and Bill (there was no Bill) want to get together with you and Barb again. When do you think you'll have the time?"

Luckily, I wasn't a complete thick-head, and I picked up on the drift at once. "Hi, Joan, good to hear from you. Look, I'm sure Barb would love to get together, but she isn't here right now. Can I call you back after I talk to her?"

"Oh darn, I'd hoped we could make some arrangements now, but I guess that's life. Look, when you two talk, just get back to Bill and me. Maybe we can meet some time at a little, intimate bar somewhere. Okay? Good talking to you, Jim. Ta ta for now." She hung up.

A little intimate bar somewhere; we had all met at the Wine Tap several times before to discuss deteriorating political and financial situations in the country. As to the reference to the "two of us," I assumed the meeting would be at two. The problem with all this intrigue was that the police were almost certainly listening in on this, and the message wasn't all that covert. Would the police or some other government agency pick up on it? Certainly when I left the house, I'll have a tail. On further consideration, it's my wife. What choice did I have? The choice was made.

Rachael and Sam needed to be picked up from school, so I called Marge to see if she could possibly pick them up. No problem, she said, but she also told me there was a strange car parked down the street. It was there at dawn and was still there. My, my, I said, that's very unsettling. You should call the police. We both laughed.

The Wine Tap only had a few patrons when I entered, but Mike, the bartender, directed me to a corner booth. The patrons in the booth had left instructions with him. Eyeing the people in the booth as I neared it, I recognized no one. My caution began to grow.

"Hi, so good to see you, Jeff!" A lady rose from her seat, smiling.

"I don't believe...." I started to say when the realization suddenly hit me. Those were Joan Bleu's eyes. My mouth started to open again, but before anything came out, Joan clamped a finger to her lips, and all the while beaming a large, broad smile out to the world.

"Have a seat, Jeff." She indicted the seat opposite her and next to someone else I didn't recognize. "Bill and I missed you and your wife lately. Haven't we, *Bill*?" Now Joan was staring at the man next to me. Looking back toward me, she continued with lowered voice, "And yes, all this is necessary."

"Darn right, old buddy." The man extended his hand. I shook it.

Next, Joan pushed a napkin across to me. "Would you like a drink? I'll call the waitress over." As she said this, she kept pushing the napkin against my hand. Looking down, I saw writing on the napkin, all in pencil. Pretending to play with it, I flipped it slightly up. It read, "You are Jeff. I am Doris and my husband is Bill. Yes, we are being watched." Reaching across the table, she pulled the paper napkin open. Inside were specific instructions on when and where to meet. And one more comment: Barbara would be there. When my drink arrived, Joan slightly jostled it, spilling all over the thin, paper napkin.

"Oh, how clumsy of me. Here, take a clean napkin." She squeezed the old napkin tightly, then nonchalantly played with it a moment, tearing the soggy mess into pieces. Then she squeezed it again into a small, tight ball. "I was so glad to hear that Barbara is okay."

A broad, straight smile was directed at me as her head bobbed up and down. "How are the kids? Have they seen their grandparents lately? You know, it's not fair to keep them away from such great grandparents. You should take the kids to visit them soon. They'll be very happy there. Even the professor thinks so. It's time." Her head was bobbing up and down again as she uttered the last words.

"I don't know. That's a big change. The kids would miss their home and friends. Are things really that...?" Trailing off, I glared at Joan with narrowed eyes.

"Jeff, it's more than time." The man - I mean Bill - interjected. "We'll be able to explain why when we get together again." He too was smiling broadly as he talked. It began to feel like I was in some silly play, but I also began to realize that it wasn't so silly anymore.

Picking Rachael and Sam up from our friends' house that evening, I told them to pack. Tomorrow morning they would be going to see grandma and grandpa for a few days. Mommy had been detained by some important business and Daddy might be joining her. Sam was excited about his little school vacation, and also because he and grandpa had some "secret traditions" that only the highly placed "Space Knights" knew about. Of course, he and grandpa were leaders of this brave, adventuresome group. Rachael, however, was older, and her apprehensive stare spoke volumes to me. Telling her not to worry, I gave her a long hug. We would all be back together soon. That was four years ago. I choked.

On my way back from dropping the kids off with Barbara's parents the next morning, I stopped at the large and busy Westside Mall. Entering the large, anchor department store I had been directed to, I went to a department that was having an enormous sale. The crowd was crushing. You couldn't see your hand in front of your face, and that was the point. Slowly, very slowly, I made my way to the employees' entrance at the rear. Attempting to enter, an employee stopped me. I told her to check with Mr. Klieman. She called on the store intercom.

After talking for a minute, she hung up and told me to go in the back and wait by the break table there. I entered and sat at a long, folding wooden table. Several employees past me questioningly going in and out. I waited. After 10 minutes, an older woman came to fetch me. As we proceeded to the mall's back employee door, I asked her if she knew what was going on? Without even turning her head toward me, she uttered, "You fool. Look at me."

Quickly, I snapped my head toward her and a familiar voice. My heart leapt as I beheld my wife, Barbara - aged about 30 years - grinning back at me.

"Pretty good makeup job, wouldn't you say, lover?"

I stopped her and turned her toward me, ready to speak.

"Not here. There are cameras everywhere." She took me by the hand and we proceeded out the back door.

Again I stopped her, and again she pulled me forward away from the building. Her other hand demurely flicked upward indicating an outside camera. Walking briskly, but not so fast that we attracted undue attention, we crossed the parking lot to a silver-colored sedan. An unseen hand opened the back door and we tumbled in. Immediately I pulled 'grandma' toward me and we shared a passionate kiss. It was then that I heard "ahhumm" from the front seat.

"While not wanting to interrupt anything, we do have some introductions to make. Then we have to get the hell out of here. Hi, my name is Jeremy."

The man in the front seat had turned toward us, grinning. He was the man who had posed as Joan Bleu's husband the night before in the bar. Now he extended his hand over the front seat. I shook it.

"Barbara and I have already met. I hope you have most of your affairs in order because we have to leave quickly before we meet some people we don't want to meet. I've just been told they're scouring the mall right now. Go, Pete."

Another man, the driver, slowly pulled out to join the traffic exiting the parking lot. Jeremy was a roughly handsome man, dark-haired and muscular, in his early thirties. He had the demeanor of military all over him. Pete, the driver, also oozed military, but more like a young recruit.

We drove through countless suburban neighborhoods and down nameless secondary roads. During the ride, Barbara asked many questions about our kids, and I assured her they were safe and well with her parents. She seemed somewhat calmed by this. Finally, we reached the edge of a state forest. Both men in front, always vigilante, now checked some sort of electronic device. Then we drove onto the narrow forest road. It was a darker, greener world. The tops of the tall trees cut out most of the sunlight save for the occasional blinding flash in small clearings.

"Are we joining Robin and his band of merry men in the forest?" I joked.

Jeremy, head half turned and grinning, replied, "Sort of."

I had to ask. "Are things really that bad? I mean, nobody is happy with what's going on in Washington, but if we win the next election...."

The Revolutionist

"Next election? You must be joking, Jim. The progressives control the elections. Have you ever noticed how they seem to win even when 90 percent of the people you talk to hate them and wouldn't vote for them if they had a gun to their heads? Oh, and speaking of guns, did you hear that our esteemed president has now banned, by executive order, all ammunition except 22 caliber bullets. You will be allowed five such bullets a year for single-shot, bolt-action rifles only. Can you say, 'Washington fears the people'?"

"I didn't hear that!" I exclaimed.

"Well, you were sort of busy and distracted, Jim. The executive action was signed this morning. It's being immediately challenged in court, but you know how that goes.

"Not to change the subject, but your wife here has become quite a celebrity. Some news organizations picked up on the school protest, her recruiting for conservative causes, and her association with Athenson. They've made her into the Patrick Henry or John Hancock of our age. On the wrong side, of course, per their warped, leftist views."

Barbara said not a word, just shook her head.

My head was swimming with all these new revelations. "My God, it sounds like we are practically in a revolution. What does Athenson have to say about all this?"

"We have no idea." Jeremy threw his head back and sighed. "We have no idea where Athenson even is. He disappeared two days ago. He knew what was coming and went into hiding. We're waiting to hear from him. He has to be *very* careful. Word is the feds are going to arrest him on sight for conspiracy, the prosecutors' darling. Then, there'll be a horrible attempt to free him by the fringe right wing, and he and all the lunatic right wingers will be killed in the process. Neat, clean, end of story."

I sat back hard, pushing my back into the seat. Barbara huddled close. Looking up, she said, "I'm so sorry, Jim. Things have gotten...."

"Sorry for what, babe? You didn't get these madmen into office. It's all those jerks, and we had no idea what they wanted to do to this country." Giving a little shudder, I sighed deeply three times.

What was going to happen to this country. My God, what could possibly be next?

*

"Lamberti, Lamberti!" A loud voice thundered. I snapped out of my far memory world. Turning my gaze to the right, I observed some officer type leading a large group of men toward me.

"Here, sir." I hailed the leader.

"Ah, Captain Lamberti."

"I'm only a sergeant, sir."

"Not anymore. You've been given a field commission all the way to captain. Congratulations."

"Thanks." I knew why they did such things. It looks good on your tombstone.

"Captain, Central Command looked over the actual number of men you have to do the tough job coming up and decided it wasn't enough. You now have a dozen more men to help get you through. These are truly tough, battle-hardened men. They will be an asset. Good luck." He shook my hand, saluted and left. I never even knew who he was.

They were tough alright. They looked like they just crawled out of an alley to knife someone. Oh, what the hell, my only concern now was that the field promotion was on official paper. On the slim chance that we actually won this thing, my kids would get better survivors' benefits.

The Revolutionist

Chapter Eight - S.C.

We actually drove through and then out of the state forest, ending up in a very rural area. The car finally drove down a dirt driveway past a sign that said Noga Dairy Farm. The truth was, I was hungry, and a silly thought flickered through my brain that a big hunk of cheese would taste pretty good right now.

The driveway was long and when we finally reached the house we didn't stop there. Circling the large, old, two-story farmhouse, we pulled directly into the barn, whose doors had been left wide open. When the car finally stopped, I noticed a man sitting in the shadowy recesses of the building. The figure rose. Half expecting to see some old man with a straw hat and a long piece of hay in his mouth, I was surprised when a svelte, muscular man of about 30 approached the car. He leaned in to talk to Pete, the driver.

"Any problems, Pete?'

"No, sir. It all went as planned."

"If only it always went that way." He peered over to Jeremy. "Good planning, major."

"Good training, sir."

Though I saw no uniforms, it was evident these people were military. But they couldn't be regular, government military or they would be in rebellion against....

"And you back there, are you all right?"

Barbara answered first. "We're fine, Colonel Farrier. It is Colonel Farrier, isn't it?"

"Yes ma'am. It's a pleasure to finally meet you, one of our top recruiters. This must be your husband, Joe."

"No colonel, my name is Jim...well James, actually."

"I'm sorry, Jim. I meet so many new faces these days. But please, come into the house, meet the others, and have something to eat. You must be tired and hungry."

"Also very curious," I said. "I hadn't realized things had gone this far."

"You have no idea, my friend; no idea."

"Do you mean...you mean," Barbara was nervously searching for words. "It might come to...some sort of violence?"

"At this point, Barbara...."

The colonel's eyes shifted to the side. He dared not look directly at her.

"Violence, rebellion, is virtually certain. Those in Washington will not give up power. No election will stop them. They'll make sure of that. They count very much on us being complacent. Day after day, they tell us the rights and freedoms we must lose to advance the country. They're making us into peasants."

Then he looked at Barbara.

"Yes, that's exactly the right word: peasants. Elections are an inconvenient formality now, perhaps to be done away with soon. Most people think of socialism as everyone being the same; no ups or downs. Well, that old socialism never worked anyway. No reason for anyone to work hard or be ambitious. But this new socialism is much more devious. Everyone's the same alright, all equal, except those at the top. They know best, so they should stay at the top. It mixes the old socialism, nobody gets anywhere, with the new socialism of 'we elites stay up here forever.'"

Farrier glanced toward the open barn door.

"The worst of all worlds. It's a new royalty, and they're the royals. But you know the worst part? The kids love it. The young lap this crap up like a religion and sell their lives for it. Oh they'll realize their mistake in twenty or thirty years, but it will be too late then."

The colonel tightened his jaw and looked at us again. "Hell, it's almost too late now."

From the outside, the farmhouse looked plain and barely inhabited. Inside, however, it looked like a Pentagon war room. It was packed with people bustling around, answering phones, checking computer monitors, reading clipboards. It was straight out of a movie.

"Unbelievable!" Barbara's mouth hung half open.

"You haven't seen any of this before?" I asked. "I thought you were part of the stop-big-government movement."

"No," Farrier answered. "Barbara was very active in raising people's awareness of the dangers and excesses of big, all-controlling government, but she was just a recruiter. Ah, let me apologize. Barbara was *the* recruiter. As such, the powers-that-be in Washington wanted her out of the way fast. They used the school demonstration as their perfect excuse. We felt we had an obligation to step in and save her. Once in custody, she would probably never have been heard from again. Further consideration included you too, Jim. We couldn't let our top recruiter's favorite man just disappear."

The colonel grinned at me.

"Oh, and we've tried to make some provision for your children. We've arranged for Barbara's parents to visit Canada, with their grandchildren of course, and have a nice, long visit. They will be safe."

Barbara squeezed my hand. Then we both thanked the colonel, but it raised the obvious question: safe from what?

Farrier took a deep breath and asked us to step into another room. It was a sort of a breakroom for everyone, but he asked those already there to leave for a few minutes. As Barb and I sat, the heavy feeling in the air was overwhelming. We knew of the worsening situation, but never really wanted to admit how truly bad it had become. Silence ruled for a few moments as we looked at Farrier and he looked down.

Finally the colonel's face came up.

"You must know what's occurring in this country. Certainly you don't like it, and most other Americans don't like it either. What's happened so far is just the beginning. Our intelligence tells us that the president, vice president, all of the cabinet, and virtually all the high appointed officers are completely devoted to transforming this nation into a strongly socialist nation. You already know of the horrific changes so far: a ruined health care system, a ruined, and strongly federally controlled, education system that just screams socialism, a greatly weakened military that makes a lot of people nervous if, God forbid, we should ever really need it. Then we have no real, practical plans for future energy supplies other than their pie-in-the-sky solar and wind. Sure you can get energy out of solar and wind systems, but at four to six times the cost of other systems, and solar and wind are notoriously unreliable. Also...."

"Stop right there, colonel." I held up my hand. "You don't have to sell us, that's why we're here. I have a question, though. About that weakened military, this place looks pretty military to me. Who are all these people?"

"Most of them are ex-military," Farrier answered. "When things truly started getting bad and it became obvious where we were being taken, Professor Athenson and five or six other 'super patriots' started contacting us and screening us to the possibility of alternate action. They got us together and presented what I can only call 'last chance' plans. These plans were basic outlines of what might be necessary if we couldn't stop them through legal means. The good professor and company left the specific plans to us. We started in earnest about two and a half years ago as things began to tumble out of control. Then, fourteen months ago, when four of our greatest enemies formed an alliance to 'crush American influence forever,' we put things in high gear. As you know, the two top terrorist states now have nuclear weapons *and* the means to deliver them. All this with no practical opposition from Washington. That's beyond comprehension!" He took a deep breath.

"Just today, in case you hadn't heard, the president, by executive action, has now banned all bullet sales to the American public. They're presenting this as a means to stop crime. Bull, you know that. Crime will always be with us. What they're really afraid of is us. Scared, that's what they are; scared of us, the public. They're scared of a rebellion, and they now have reason to be."

"Can I...can I take it for granted then that there really will be an armed opposition...rebellion?" I almost spat the word out.

"Damn right, Mr. Lamberti. We're not here for the fun of it."

"Colonel, I'd like to talk to Professor Athenson. I have a very good rapport with him and since, as you said, he started all this, I assume he may be...I don't know, the leader?"

"You can do more than assume. He *is* the leader, but you still can't talk to him."

"Oh, power gone to his head, has it?" I interjected.

The colonel grinned. "I wouldn't know. No one would know. No one knows where he is. A few days ago one of our intelligence people intercepted a secret government memo to 'pick him up for intensive and lengthy questioning.' You know what that means. Joan Bleu was also mentioned in the memo. A day later, so were you, Barbara. Athenson has completely disappeared. He'll contact us when he feels it necessary. Last night we got Joan and a couple of others away just before the feds arrived. The screws are really tightening. Any day, any minute now - snap!"

Barb and I looked at each other. What do you say when you realize your country is about to explode into war; real war?

"So," I turned toward Farrier, "You guys are here preparing your plans for war and rebellion?"

"No!" Farrier glanced sideways to me, "Everyone out there is preparing to get out of here in a hurry. We are 99 percent sure they have almost made our location. We have to be out of here in three hours. Care to join us?"

Three loud, strong raps on the door, and a 'come in' from the colonel.

"Sorry, sir, but you'll want to check the TV monitor immediately." Some sort of orderly addressed Farrier nervously. Before the orderly or Farrier could move, I leaned over and turned up the sound on the TV, which had been on, but with the sound down, no one paid attention to it.

"The mob has gotten out of control in the streets." The announcer on the set bellowed. "What they claimed would be a peaceful demonstration has turned into ugly, deadly rioting."

"We were afraid of this." Farrier jaw tightened. "Two groups were supposed to hold a combined, peaceful demonstration today in Washington." The National Gun Association and the Committee for Constitutional Rights were combining forces in a march on the Supreme Court and the capitol. Neither were armed nor planning any trouble, just a very large demonstration. We tried to warn them that the government itself might start something and blame it on them. They took the chance."

The TV continued, "Half way through the march, many marchers produced Molotov cocktails and threw them at police lines. Next, they produced guns and started firing. Our heroic government forces had no choice but to return fire on these traitorous morons. Our news people, located in several spots, have so far counted at least thirty bodies, and the number is rising. Most of these bodies are of our brave government servants trying to protect our treasured national institutions. May God bless them."

Farrier exploded

"I'm gonna vomit. Those poor bastards weren't armed! There wasn't so much as a fire cracker among them! They wanted the big boys to know they were sick of the increasing government control of everything and everyone, but specifically, they didn't want to make trouble. This is murder!"

Barbara flipped forward in her seat and shot her hand up to silence the colonel. "Listen!" she hissed.

"I will repeat that." The TV commentator continued, "The leader of this atrocious attack on Washington, one Professor Athenson, has been captured hiding in a small cabin in the Ozark Mountains section of Missouri. With him were two other

94

traitorous turncoats as yet unidentified. These cowardly rebels, it was reported, didn't even put up a fight." The commentator smirked, "They hid while their people died."

Colonel Farrier fairly shook with rage. "He had no part of that demonstration other than to tell them not to go! He told them things had gone too far in Washington and it might well be dangerous."

I then asked the colonel, "What do we do?"

"We get the hell out of here fast!"

*

"Okay? Do you understand our prime objective? If we can do this, there's still a very good chance we can win. Any questions?" Only one hand went up.

"Yeah? Can I knife as many of those pretty boys as I can reach on our way there?" Then he laughed, followed by all of his new cohorts. What was that thought I'd had earlier about these guys crawling out of an alley with knives? Well, such is war and the people and situations that mold it. I told them to eat their extra rations now and grab a nap. It wouldn't be long.

Sitting down myself, Gil approached me. "Well, sir, they look tough because they are. Honestly, that's what's needed. We might just have an actual chance of doing this if the main column can open up a big enough gap."

"Maybe," I agreed, "and what's this 'sir' stuff?"

"Captain Lamberti, sir. You're an officer now!"

"Oh, crap. That's right."

Gil produced a cigarette and handed it to me. "I thought we were out. I've never seen anyone that could come up with smokes the way you can."

"It's a talent, *sir*." Gil smiled at me.

Though not able to sleep myself, I felt the men of my unit needed some rest before this conclusive operation. They needed to be strong and alert, certainly not groggy. Just as I watched most of their eyes giving in to sleep, the entire line exploded into shouts, quickly followed by small-arms fire. Everyone was up now and instinctively grabbing their weapons.

Just as a myriad of cautious looks went above the berm, I saw one trooper in a unit down the line to my immediate left raise his weapon only to have his buddy suddenly push him to deflect the shot. The new shouts were, "Don't shoot! don't shoot!"

Looking out myself, I saw the outline of a figure running furiously from government lines and waving a flag as he ran. The spotlights that promptly appeared from the government side clearly outlined him, but they also made it impossible to identify him in any way. In fact, you couldn't even tell if it was a "him."

Two things that did come into focus, though, the flag he waved was white, and he didn't appear to be armed. Fire from the federal troops, at first wild, was now centering in. The figure made it to within 10 feet or so from our lines, then at least two powerful shots struck him, whirling his body around and pushing him another 5 feet. Now we could see him. I'd moved 50 yards over to the spot he almost made it to. Government fire had ceased. They'd got him.

No, he was still alive! We could hear him breathing hard and moaning slightly. The same guy who had raised his weapon to kill him now impulsively went over the berm top to grab his hand and pull him back. Before the other side could resume fire, our guy had dragged him back and down behind the berm with the help of others.

The man, and it was a man, wasn't good. At least one massive hole through his chest was pouring blood. Somebody tried to apply pressure to the wound to stop the hemorrhaging. Two others propped his head up and tried to give him some water, but gobs of blood were now trickling out of his mouth. Despite all this, he tried to talk. We couldn't understand him at first. I noticed the name on his uniform, PFC Salazar. Several of us now bent down close to his mouth to hear whatever it was that he thought important enough to sacrifice his life for.

"They...lie. Don't care 'bout people. Power, power with them. Bad. Don't let...them take you. Fight or die."

He stopped to cough up more blood and gulp in more breaths. He was in agony and I pitied him. This 'former enemy' who had undoubtedly killed many of our guys, now lay dying himself to deliver a message to us.

"Tanks - brought in almost a hundred. They...to lead the charge at dawn." Gasping for air, he tried to continue. "Jets will come. Tanks in front, jets behind you. All at dawn. They're tired of the game. Want it ended. Dawn is your doom."

Even I looked away from the massive ejection of blood from his mouth. "Fight...fight to last. Don't let them...ahhhh."

A sickening last gasp and shudder ran through his body. His frame stiffened, then slowly relaxed. Someone reached over and brought his eyelids down. The fight, regardless of side, was over for him.

"Well, sir? What do you think? Was he telling the truth?" Some unknown grunt piped up.

Still looking at Salazar's body, I replied, "People tend not to sacrifice their lives for lies, soldier."

"Yes, sir, but they could have fed him a bunch of crap, then got him mad, and...."

"It's possible, soldier, but it's not my call." Fixing my eyes on the grunt now, I ordered, "Get your ass over to headquarters *now*. Ask for General Ordway. Tell them Captain Lamberti has sent an urgent message, verbal only, for the general's ears exclusively, and tell him what happened here. If they won't let you see him, tell them Captain Lamberti will be back with all his men to deliver the message, and the captain won't be in a good mood. Now move it."

The young soldier jumped up and away in a flash.

I'd heard rumors before that the feds had drafted every Hispanic they could and that they were giving them all the dirtiest and most dangerous jobs. Then, even after they proved themselves, they chided them with threats of "do more" and "be braver" or we'll send you back to beans-and-rice land. I guess those things weren't just rumors. Damn feds. They promise the world, but when it comes to actually delivering, they fall short every time.

Several of us dragged Salazar's body a few yards behind the front line and covered it with a thin plastic tarp weighted down with heavy pieces of wood.

Walking back to my unit, I couldn't help but think that Salazar probably just got better treatment than I would get when I fell. For some reason, I laughed at that. My attention now turned to what he'd said. If true, it changed the whole picture, and not for the best. Could we do anything? Would we do anything? I sat to ponder and wait. The wait wasn't long.

"Captain!" Gil's voice.

I picked my head up.

"They say General Ordway's coming."

Trying to rise quickly, it all hit me. My knees hurt, my hips hurt, my back hurt, and a waive of exhaustion swept over me. I wasn't 19 anymore - or even 29. I pushed my thoughts aside.

"Captain Lamberti, what happened here?" Ordway didn't look too spry himself, yet he pushed on.

"General, didn't you get my man's report?"

Ordway came right up into my face. "Got it, Jim, but this is something I need more input on, and more details if you've got them."

We went over what the dead federal soldier had said and how truthful we thought it might be.

Amazingly, we agreed that, whether he lied or not, we had no choice. We couldn't just sit here and wait to be slaughtered. Now it was just a matter of timing. It would definitely be best to go before dawn to beat the tanks and the jets, but if we went too early, the presidential helicopter wouldn't land, and wasn't that the whole purpose of our last, best push?

"Forty-five minutes before dawn, Jim. I think that'll do it. The tank crews will be just in early prep and the jets will still be far enough away. The chopper wanted to land early anyway. If it's not quite down yet, I think we can force it down and keep it here. News flash, captain, we got two new laser weapons. One doesn't work right and neither of them is very powerful. But if we start firing them over the chopper, they will be reluctant to rise and flee. The laser might not destroy them, but if it hit and damaged their rotor, no telling what might happen to them. I think it will force them to land at that point. Once on the ground - if you make it - we win.

"Another thing you should know, captain. We have an ace in the hole on board. Can't tell you more now, Jim, but if that damn thing touches down, that's it."

General Ordway's right thumb was up.

"We'll be ready, sir. Forty-five minutes before dawn."

"I know you will, Jim. I never had any doubts." He looked down, then up again. "You've been an outstanding soldier, Jim. You've accomplished everything demanded of you, sometimes at great personal sacrifice and pain. But this...this is it. If you and your team make it, we win. If not...." He sighed. "That's a hell of a burden to put on your shoulders, captain, but you were the almost unanimous pick."

"Almost, sir? I'd like to know who voted against me."

Ordway laughed, saluted me, then grabbed my hand and shook it. Turning, he walked away at a brisk pace, hailing men as he went. Suddenly I had the oddest feeling that I would never see this man again. I shook it off.

Chapter Nine - N.H.

"We have solid intelligence that we've been made and this location has been compromised. That's why the frantic pace."

Major Jeremy was throwing old paper notebooks into a large box.

"We back up all computer work with good old, solid paper. In fact, most of our really important stuff is only paper. Hackers can't crack the codes and pick up all our secrets from some remote location. Hey, how about a hand here. Take those boxes and find a trunk to put them in."

Barbara took one box and I picked up another, or tried to. The box I grabbed weighed a ton. It was impossible to move. Another guy put down his box and came over to help me.

"I'll help you, buddy. Name is Steve."

"Thanks, Steve. I'm Jim. Just what's in this box anyway?"

As we began to move it slowly toward the door, Steve answered. "It's full of hand grenades, friend. We'll give those government wonks a warm reception if they show up early."

My jaw dropped.

It dropped again as we exited the building. Outside were at least thirty vehicles of every shape and size. They hadn't been there just 20 minutes before. Steve explained they only wanted to use cars and SUV's, civilian-type vehicles. Trucks would attract too much attention.

Everything from that old farmhouse was cleaned out in 10 more minutes, and I joined Barb in the car we had ridden in before. Pete was there again, but not Jeremy. Three minutes later, Jeremy came running out and jumped in the car. He waved an arm in the air and our caravan took off down the long driveway. Once we reached the road, the group split in two different directions. At first we burned rubber with our speed, but at the next intersection we slowed down and our smaller group split again.

Barbara broke the silence. "Jeremy, I assume we're all going to the same place?"

"Absolutely, ma'am, but obviously by different roads. We don't even know *where* we're going. Each vehicle has different coded directions, and the final destination isn't named. Sit back and enjoy. Point of interest. Did you notice that I was a few minutes late? Reason was, I was getting a phone call from one of our internal operatives. There are protests all over the country about what happened in Washington. You won't hear about the protests on the news, though. The government-friendly media isn't covering it. They don't want to embarrass their friends and cohorts in Washington. Some of the protests were pretty rough. A lot of protesters didn't make it."

"They can't cover up stuff like that. It's got to get out eventually." I was incensed.

"Oh, it's getting out alright. We have a telephone network set up and, failing that, a backup shortwave network. It's already all over the country. Not a word, though, on regular network TV news. Per those morons, Washington is just doing its usual good, patriotic duty, humming along, and a few foolish, conservative rock-throwers have been taken into custody in some widely scattered cities. Nothing to see here. Move along."

I continued, "What about the Internet? Spread it all over the 'Net."

"Have you not been paying attention?" Jeremy smirked as his head turned back to me. "The 'Net has been under government control for years now. You don't seriously believe them when they tell you they don't tap and control computer content, do you?"

Barb and I just stared at each other.

"Hey, any word on Athenson?" Barbara's face showed concern.

"No, but we have people working on it." Jeremy sighed and looked down.

The Revolutionist

"Who's running the show then, Jeremy?"

"Well, right now.......I guess Joan Bleu is. She's the only central person not in government custody right now. Of course there's Ordway."

"Who's Ordway?" Barb and I asked in concert.

"General Ordway. He was the guy forced out of the military a few years ago by 'our esteemed president.' Remember? A great general, but he wasn't in synch with the new socialist policies in Washington. They skinned him alive in public and on TV. You must remember the almost continuous media coverage of his hearings. He was a true patriot and very competent. The poor guy didn't deserve any of it."

"Oh yes, I do remember," I replied.

Suddenly the old TV coverage came back to me. Ordway had been very successful overseas. Too successful, actually, for the almost traitorous regime in our capital, which wanted us to fail. They wanted the other side to win because, as many said, in far too many areas those in charge seemed to agree with our enemies rather than our western alliance. After all, The U.S. had to be brought down and humiliated publicly on the world stage.

"So he is...." Barbara started.

"Well, we're not sure. Right now we're sort of operating on momentum. But Joan has told us to watch out for 'events.'" Jeremy threw his head back and closed his eyes.

I wished I could have closed mine, but my mind was racing.

*

"Sir, you really should try and get some rest. It won't be long now." Gil had sneaked up and stood over me.

"Yes, mother. You know, Gil, you really are older than your years. After this thing is over and we return to regular human life, I'm going to make sure you get married. You'd make a great father *and* mother."

"Ha! Very funny, Grandpa sir!"

"Sit down, Gil. Neither of us is going to get any sleep tonight." Gil flopped down beside me. "I guess we both know the odds. We should appreciate every moment now."

"Yeah, but I still want my vengeance ."

"Humph. Got any cigarettes, Gil?"

"Those things will kill you, Captain." Again we snickered. "Actually, no. This time I finally ran out." He gave a loud sigh.

We sat silently for an unknown time, staring upward to catch glimpses of the stars peeking through the bright night clouds. Gil broke first.

"So after this is over, you goin' north to Canada to collect your kids?"

"Darn right. I really miss...." The words stuck in my throat. I couldn't talk.

"Yeah, I hear Canada's really beautiful. My mom and dad always wanted to take this train through some mountains out in western Canada. They...." Now Gil's voice stopped.

I began to think of Gil as almost another son in just the short time I'd known him. He was a smart, moral young man who had loved his family. He deserved better, but who didn't?

"It's snowin', it's snowin'!" Both our heads snapped up as voices were raised all along the line.

"What the....?" Gil started to jump up. I held him back.

"Don't blow it now, Gil. Keep your head down."

Out of the black night sky huge flakes began falling. It wasn't snow, though, it was a barrage of pamphlets. There must have been tens of thousands of them. As I picked one up, I could see the large federal seal at the top. Reading the message, I snorted.

It read: "Don't throw your life away. Surrender now and know the mercy of your still caring, benevolent government. Don't forget those at home who want to see you again. Amnesty Guaranteed."

I could hear Marvin Taylor shouting down the line. "Yeah, once the bullet passes through your head, they definitely won't bring you to trial." That was the general reaction from everyone. They knew the score, and I knew the reason. The feds were probably filming this right now. Something they could show on TV tomorrow night after their expected victory. It was one last, merciful chance for these terrorist rebels, they would claim, by the most merciful federal government.

I crumpled the leaflet. Then, picking up my weapon, I raised it over the berm and cut loose three rounds toward government lines. That was repeated by a thousand others. So much for their offer of mercy.

*

It was dark and drizzly when Barb, I and the rest arrived at our new home. The weather, like my mood, wasn't very good, but the irony of where we were did make me laugh a bit. New rebel headquarters -- yes, I guess we were officially rebels now -- was located in a warehouse behind a large shopping mall outside of Richmond, Virginia. Ironic: Richmond had been the rebel capital during the Civil War almost 200 years ago.

We were able to drive right into the enormous warehouse. Even after driving in, however, nothing damning could be seen. Down the center section of the large building there were only stacked packing crates on each side; two virtual mountain ranges of such crates that completely blocked any view of what was on the other sides.

There were directors inside who showed us exactly where to park. Once parked, we were told where to deposit the boxes we had brought. On the other side of those two high mountain ranges of crates were two long lines of large tents, one on each side. These were special tents that kept the light in, so no light could creep out and be seen, and were made of a special, thick material that discouraged radar penetration and thus detection. Now it really began to sink in as to my country's precarious position, and the side I was on.

DeEarlon

After initial setup, we were all called into a small shed-type building within the warehouse. This shed was intelligence central.

We received coffee and energy bars while waiting for the kitchen to be finished at the other end of the main building. That's when everyone present received further distressing news. Our enemies in Europe, the Middle East and Asia were moving. Being in the middle of our own potential war, we really hadn't had time to think much about global affairs. Europe was a mess. Turkey had fallen to the Caliphate of Iran, which now threatened central Europe directly. Not to be outdone, the terrorist army in Spain had just won a major victory over the combined European army. Everyone knew this terrorist army was yet another extension of the mighty Iranian Caliphate.

To the north, Russian forces had reclaimed much of their old Soviet empire. Western Poland and the far west of the Czech Republic were the only holdouts. Free Europe was being crushed.

Asia was no better. China had taken over Taiwan with a massive loss of life, then gone on to a naval blockade of Japan. India and Australia were sending naval forces to try and lift the blockade, but India had its own problems. Threatened on the north by China and by a renewed invasion on the west from Pakistan, now under the control of the immensely powerful Iranian Caliphate. Korea, we were told, had virtually ceased to exist. North and South Korea had eliminated each other.

The surprise, I suppose, was Latin America. Socialists centered in Venezuela and Cuba had sparked followers in Bolivia, Peru, and Nicaragua into a continent-wide war. Brazil, Argentina, and Colombia had responded, but Colombia fell fast. Chile and Mexico were trying to negotiate a peace, but both had internal revolts of their own.

World chaos. No one, particularly those idiots in Washington, had truly appreciated the former position of the United States in keeping world peace. Yes, it had been precarious and expensive,

The Revolutionist

but it had worked.

When America pulled all serious backing from our former allies, all hell broke loose. We already knew what had happened to Israel when a former administration, a precursor to our present geniuses, had pulled all support for the Jewish state. It was sickening. With Russian help, it had only taken twelve days for Israel to disappear. There had been a short nuclear exchange, but the Russian arsenal was overwhelming. Now Iran held a small, captive cadre of Jews which it showed off to the world as proof of its mercy. Word had it that these poor souls were required weekly to announce publicly how they loved their Iranian overlords. If they refused a public announcement ... the unthinkable!

Saudi Arabia had fallen. Mecca was now in Shite hands, which precipitated a slaughter throughout the Near and Middle East. Egypt was about to surrender to the growing might of the Iranian Caliphate. Iran now had nuclear weapons, and lots of them.

"What about Canada? What's going on there?" Barbara was almost out of her seat.

There was no word on Canada. No word now was probably good at this time. Our eyes met and our hearts raced. I reached out to hold her hand, tightly. Other words were said from the experts briefing us, but neither of us listened. My mind and Barb's were filled with visions of Rachael and Sam.

Later that night we and several others received our first appointments. We would start formal training in the morning. Training would have to be fast because things were moving fast. Ex-military recruited by Athenson were in charge, but the bulk of the force was civilian. It appeared, should it come to violence, that it would be poorly trained civilians against a professional army.

Hardly fair, but we were devoted to that dream that once existed here: freedom. The great hope, of course, was that the military, or most of it, would back the people. That's what they were supposed to do; back their country and the people of their country. But would they? Over the centuries, most rebellions against a powerful central government had failed, unless the military had turned to back the citizens. That is always the hope, and hope is what you live on.

The next morning, firearms were distributed. It was a random affair initially. Everyone received training on both rifles and handguns, but what was actually assigned to you was largely first-come, first-served. Word was that more were on the way. Updated versions and enough for all, we prayed. The government, fearful of the public for decades now, had been systematically seizing all weapons. Then there was ammunition, which the government tried to eliminate entirely. Most was either smuggled in now or made in an ever-growing network of home basement factories.

At dinner on the second night, we heard news of the political dam starting to burst. Riots were occurring everywhere over strict and expensive government policies. Reports even said some rioters screamed, "unconstitutional."

That was amazing, a few had listened! The government was losing patience. Security forces used tear gas and rubber bullets at first. Then, in Chicago, police backed up by National Guard forces opened up with real bullets. Was it an accident? Was it fear on the part of the official forces being pressed hard by an enormous crowd. We'll never know, but we do know that two dozen rioters were killed as they turned and ran. Early the next morning, rioters returned to burn police stations and the National Guard encampment. It was inevitable, or as Professor Athenson had said, under the circumstances, a historic certainty.

You worry. You worry about your family and friends; about your home and your hometown; about the future. Occasionally, a fleeting memory of a once quiet, orderly life would sneak in. Soon, however, you learn to worry about your own skin. At that point, bravado, determination and brotherhood are what carry you on.

The Revolutionist

The stories were endless now. There were demonstrations in every state, most being met with real bullets as the government no longer masked its anger. But the people's anger also grew. The rebels received an interesting shortwave report from the small town of Derby, Vermont. Thousands of U.S. citizens had driven north on Interstate 91 to pass into Canada to escape the violence.

This angered the government in Washington, which ordered the Vermont National Guard to set up a roadblock to stop the exodus. Three hundred guard soldiers were ordered to Derby, but only ninety actually showed up. The confrontation between, on one side, those leaving and the town's people, and, on the other side, the guardsmen, became a much-repeated story all across the U.S. northern border.

The guardsmen were driven back by those trying to leave. These escapees were aided by the people of Derby. Even more disturbing for government officials, many un-uniformed guardsmen came to back the escaping citizens and the people of the town. None of this was reported by the national media, of course, but the word got around. Confidence began to grow among rebels and rebel sympathizers.

The president went on television several times pleading for peace and calm, but conditions only worsened. Few liked him, or his policies. Washington then turned to several popular Progressive Party governors and senators. Still the trouble continued.

What followed, however, was the true beginning of the full-scale revolution. The president convinced several high-ranking Conservative Party members, his opponents, to appear on television and appeal for peace. This did not go as planned. The cry of, "How dare they, the traitors!" was heard from shore to shore.

Now the Conservative leaders were enemies too; just as bad as the Progressives in the eyes of most people. The nation exploded.

DeEarlon

The regular armed forces were called in. It was all-out war.

General Ordway finally joined the group outside Richmond. Ordway had been busy stealthily setting up potential resistance armies all across the nation and contacting sympathetic regular military leaders to join the rebels if necessary. His efforts were about to be tested.

Government forces were not idle either. While preparing militarily for a civil war, they also began to pressure an "ace in the hole" they possessed. Professor Athenson was pressured daily to go on national media and tell his followers to stop the violence and submit to government authority. Despite resisting at first, psychologists using powerful, mind-altering drugs eventually got Athenson to record a message of surrender to the public. Few were fooled, though, as the rebels sent out word of the drugs they suspected the government had used. Mobs, now more organized under rebel leadership, not only continued to attack government facilities and units, but began gaining significant ground.

Things began to look very good for the rebels, and the powers in Washington grew extremely nervous.

As the weeks passed, we continued our training. A clandestine message was received from Canada. It was in code, from Barb's parents, assuring us that all was well with the family. Both of us could breath a little easier.

We also met some interesting people while in training. I met a fiery pastor named Will, whose simple explanation as to why he was there was that, during the original American Revolution, most pastors backed the revolutionaries from their pulpits. Pastor Will's position was: Could he, in good conscience, do any less today for the good of the people?

Barb met Rabbi Berkowitz from Pennsylvania who, for the most part, gave the same explanation. Rabbi Berkowitz added, however, that Washington's backstabbing of Israel and its eventual demise was also a powerful incentive to fight on the rebel side.

"You see, hon, God is on our side," Barbara proudly beamed one evening.

"I hope so, babe. I really hope so."

At the end of eight weeks, we each got our assignments. I was attached to the Freedom Fighters, First Patriot Army as a sergeant. We would operate between Boston and Richmond. Barb was attached to the First Advanced Intelligence Group, whose job it was to gather military intelligence and field reports in the same general area. Hopefully we would meet some time. And we did.

As we left, several thousand new recruits straggled in. They had to be very careful not to attract undue attention. Until the third round of recruits was trained, armed and ready to fight, command felt it could not possibly defend its central position. That turned out to be true.

Chapter Ten - Va.

It's the waiting. The waiting drives you crazy. Most people don't realize it, but it isn't battle that's the worst part of war. In battle you're too busy and preoccupied to be nervous, think about your life, your family, and what might be coming. In the chaos of battle, you just react according to your training and experience. That, considering the business you're engaged in, is a good thing. But while you're *waiting* for battle, oh God, the weight of thought and memory all hits you.

No one could really sleep. There wasn't a person here who didn't know the odds. Dead, dead in a few hours, so enjoy the short time left. Most, I'm sure, were thinking of loved ones and what might happen to those loved ones if we lost. That's a powerful incentive not to lose. Even if you die, kill as many of them as you can for the victory of your side and, just maybe, those you love may live.

Some just wanted revenge. They had been fighting a long time and had seen so many of their friends die, they wanted to even the score. They were out to kill the other side, plain and simple. Nothing would stop them; no fear, no pain. That was Gil. When you're so young and you watch your family being slaughtered, there is but one thing left on your mind..

Money, your standard of living, opportunities for advancement; all the things we used to take for granted had been crushed by the present regime. They had promised much, but what they had delivered was destruction of the middle class. The middle class was the backbone of America, and they had broken it.

Enormous, overwhelming change; those in Washington were forcing such change in every sector of the nation. Bringing in millions of illegal immigrants and showering them with benefits and jobs at the cost of born, bred and tax-paying citizens. To add more sour to the mash, these new arrivals refused to learn our language and customs. They insisted on us learning *their* ways. This went for religion as well. Right or wrong, the Muslim world seemed to be mocking us and, amazingly, our leaders gave full shift to this apparent downplay of our religions at the gain of the followers of Mohammed. Sour grapes plus and mounting!

Then there were the true patriots. I know, we were all supposed to be patriots, and we were. It's just that, for some, it was the premier reason. They cried, actually cried, at the disdain those in Washington had for the Constitution, the supreme law of our land. As they saw each day, the government seized more power at the expense of the people and the people's power, rights and freedom. A free country must be free. We were once the freest country on Earth, and that must not die, even if many of us do.

All these reasons and more, I'm sure, accounted for the presence of these men and women - these rebels and revolutionists, the ones who now sat and waited with me.

I'd heard an expression from colonial times that fit this complicated situation perfectly. It went something like "putting fire to powder."

Yes - fire to powder. It was perfect!

Ah, and what about you, Jimmy boy? Why were *you* here? I thought a moment before looking up. Then, with a rueful smile, I murmured, "I guess all of the above, and you too babe. Oh yes, you too."

Puckering my lips, I sent a small kiss heavenward. Noticing a couple of the new men staring at me, I turned my head as a tiny tear made its way down my cheek.

A small whirring sound suddenly caught everyone's ear. It came and went quickly. Though you couldn't see it, they all knew exactly what it was. A tiny government drone had passed straight down the line over them, checking things out. Something was about to happen. Sure enough, within a couple of minutes, federal artillery opened up. They were softening us up for the final assault. I snickered as I watched the shells falling and exploding a good fifty to sixty yards behind their line. Everyone noted it. There was little fear in the line about these shells. They knew well that the feds wanted them alive for publicity reasons. The Freedom Fighters were to be marched in chains through the capital before execution. The feds must be shaking with excited anticipation.

I was also sure that about two or three miles straight in front of me, a helicopter was approaching. That chopper contained a very special cargo. The noise of the artillery covered the chopper sound perfectly.

*

"He's free, he's free!" The call echoed through the immense building.

I was just packing my duffle and about to go say good-bye to Barbara. Everyone rushed out into the main corridor. The question of "Who's free?" drifted throughout. And the answer; "Athenson escaped, he escaped!"

The cheers were deafening!

I turned toward Barbara, who was behind me. She was gone. Pushing my way through the throng, I circled the area we'd been in. No Barbara. Finally shrugging my shoulders, I returned to the tent we shared. As I finished packing, a familiar voice boomed behind me.

"Jim, did you hear?" It was Barb.

Turning, I boomed back. "Where were you?".

"Oh, sorry, hon. I took off to find someone who knew the score. I ran into Colonel Farrier. You know how Athenson escaped?"

"Obviously not." My irritation still radiated.

"I'm sorry, Jim. Really." She came over and squeezed my hand. "It's just that I was so excited and curious." Now her excitement stepped up two notches at least.

"Listen to this. I don't know who they were, but one of the head staff who was taken prisoner with Athenson managed to get a message out, begging to be saved. They were; and you won't believe by whom!"

Dramatic silence as she paused and grinned at me.

Throwing my hands up, I grinned back. "Okay, I give up. Who?"

"A special forces unit! A *government* special forces unit. They turned, Jim. They turned!"

This truly was good news and I knew it. We had all been hoping that regular military would turn and support the people. Without it, we really didn't think we had a chance. But something else occurred to me just then.

"You know, this could have been a trick. They could have been setting Athenson up to lead the feds to central command."

"Athenson is no fool, hon. You should know that by now. He insisted that he and his friends be set free before they reached anyone of importance. He told them, the special forces unit, to wait in a certain place and, once he and friends were safe, he'd contact them to tell them where to report. They did it, and we're ahead of the game. Jim, this wasn't just seven or eight guys. It was the whole unit, sixty or seventy! God, with special forces, that's like an army."

Barbara was glowing. It was like we'd already won the conflict. If only we had both known what was to come.

A second thought popped into my head then, one that we'd lightly perused before.

"Hon, how are we communicating? You're in intelligence and you must know. I mean, we can't pick up a phone, not even a cell phone. We can't really use the Internet. I don't think we're using the telegraph, and I haven't noticed any smoke signals lately."

Now she looked down sheepishly. "Jim, we've discussed this before. You know I can tell you nothing, just in case...." An awkward pause stopped her. "There are other ways to instantly communicate. Eventually, you'll know, but...."

Now it was my turn to hold her hands. "I know, hon, and I

know it's a matter of life and death, but I just thought, maybe..."
A silly smirk crossed my face.

"You'll know soon enough." She reached up and kissed me.

The news of Athenson's escape spread fast, by any means of communication. Within eight hours, and without media help, it was across the nation. An electric shock ran through the populace. Some neighborhoods went into lockdown while others held parties, parties not unnoticed by the authorities. Twenty four hours after the escape, the United States of America was in a state of siege. Riots by giant mobs rolled across the landscape. Murders, burnings, police stations under attack; this time there was no holding it back.

It was a true civil war, but not as much on a geological base as it had been in the 1860s. This was more a philosophical/political rift. Most who believed in strong government control, i.e. socialism, lived in the Northeast and on the West Coast. Most who believed in individual liberty and constitutional government lived in the South and Midwest.

Almost every place, however, was split. Street battles occurred in virtually every city, large and small, across the country. The police couldn't help. They themselves were being attacked. Federal and state authorities called out every military and paramilitary organization they could.

There were two effects of this call-up. First, it became evident that the crowds were uncontrollable unless extreme measures were used. Measures that led to large-scale bloodshed. Next, to the authorities' horror, many soldiers, full or part time, did not report for duty. All appeared in chaos. Then it got worse; or better, depending on your outlook.

Five days after the news of Athenson's escape reached the whole nation, actual war began. General Ordway, noting the federal government's preoccupation with riot control, launched a full-scale attack on Washington, D.C., while simultaneously calling on the president and Congress to surrender and resign.

The Revolutionist

Of course, no resignations happened.

The reason General Ordway could launch an attack was that he had already arranged for most of a full Marine Corps unit and two National Guard units sympathetic to the rebel cause to lead the charge.

I was in the rear of this advance with the newly organized First Division, American Freedom Fighters. While there was stiff resistance from military units assigned to protect Washington, our sheer numbers eventually overwhelmed them. It also helped that Ordway persuaded two Air Force squadrons to have engine trouble, so there was little air support for the capital. There was, however, a lot of missile and drone cover. We lost most of our people in the battle to drones and missiles.

I had never been in battle before. Despite training and preparation, it was an education. For a civilian soldier, it turned out to be a hard and often shocking education. To actually be there, to see death and participate in it, was sometimes shocking, sickening, and numbing. You do your duty though, just as you were trained. One thing you learn early, if you don't follow through, you wind up as one of the dead.

After this battle, the First Battle of Washington, General Ordway had all the government missile and drone unit commanders brought before him. They all thought they were going to be shot, but Ordway actually commended them on their bravery and dedication to duty despite their personal feelings. Surprised, several of these officers actually switched sides on the spot. It was a proud moment for rebel forces.

Not all our forces were so successful. American Freedom Fighters won another battle in Georgia, but we were only holding our own in most places. North of New York City we were losing, and losing badly. Our commander there, General Marteen, had been killed in the initial attack on assembled federal forces there, and his second in command was completely incompetent. Our patriot forces were running north on the Hudson and being slaughtered as they ran. The West Coast wasn't much better. Out there, messy stand-offs and stalemates were the order of the day. We heard a rumor, hard to confirm, that the Air Force Academy in Colorado Springs was on our side. Again, we prayed that was true.

Still, we had Washington, and that was a major accomplishment. The political bigwigs there were astonished. Almost to a person, none of them could believe this was possible. The Progressive Party leaders were scared to death, and with good reason. We all learned within the first 48 hours of capturing the city, exactly what the rush had been. That 'amazing, but secret' communications system that Barb and I had been previously discussing turned up something disgusting one month earlier.

Virtually every Progressive Party leader was a quisling, an internal traitor to their own land and people. Secrets turned up proving their clandestine negotiations to turn over large portions of our Southwest to Mexican sympathizers. Whether the government of Mexico knew about this or not wasn't really clear in the documents recovered, but many leading Latin multimillionaires knew. In fact, they financed the scheme. They, no doubt, would be the leaders of this new nation. It would have established a quasi independent Latin nation out of Southern California, Nevada, Arizona, New Mexico, part of Texas, and part of Colorado.

There would be "private," and very large, remuneration to Progressive Party leaders. This was treason on a massive scale. Not only were these leeches trying to turn our nation into a socialist state, they were trying to sell part of it. And it got worse! The scheme started with the Progressives, but it seems at least a few of the Conservatives knew about it as well. When a few of the Conservative leaders confronted their Progressive counterparts, they too were offered massive amounts of money. They took the money, and plans were made to justify the upcoming national surprise by saying such a change was probably inevitable anyway. Thickening the plot, it seems the conspirators informed the left-leaning members of the Supreme Court, now numbering seven, to make sure the nation was informed that such a division was indeed legal.

Most of the Freedom Fighters' army leaders wanted them all shot at once, but cooler, more just heads prevailed.

Athenson had made his way into Washington through scattered and chaotic federal lines. After appearing triumphantly before the Freedom Fighters, he and General Ordway convened. First they assessed exactly who they had in custody. Among the honored guests were the vice president, both parties' leaders in the Senate and House of Representatives, the attorney general and his two top assistants, all Supreme Court justices, and the head of the FBI. They were furious to find the president, plus entourage, had escaped on a stealth helicopter only twelve hours before the city fell.

The same secret information that had uncovered the traitorous plot to sell off part of the country clearly showed who was involved. The president and all the leaders they had in custody were guilty, with three exceptions. The leader of the House Conservatives and the two conservative Supreme Court justices seemed to be out of the loop. They were dismissed. A trial was announced for the others, a mass treason trial!

Still, the big fish had escaped. That "slimy dog," as Ordway called the president, had slipped the net using decoy helicopters to cover his escape. Both Athenson and Ordway vowed to eventually bring him to justice. This pledge became consistently stronger as the treason trials progressed. It came out during these trials that over the last few years enormous transfers of money had taken place from public coffers to "secret accounts" of these powerful people.

Even worse, any poor soul in government or out, who "might have" even suspected what was going on, disappeared one way or another. For what had once been regarded as an honest, representative republic, these revelations were stomach-turning. The military court found them all guilty of treason, complicit in multiple murders, and, worst of all, undermining the very foundations of our free republic. All were sentenced to be hanged.

There would be one, mass public execution. For what they had done to this land and its people, there would be no mercy.

The trials had taken only two weeks. The executions took place two days after the trials ended. The military court ordered the president back for trial. He declined. In fact, he was busy trying to countermand both the trials and their conclusions; and raising forces against the Freedom Fighters.

While all this was going on, my fortunes took a temporary upturn. Barbara had been ordered into Washington as part of the team that uncovered most of this illegal and treasonous information. My wife and I had a long-overdue reunion. For a while, there was no war. Unfortunately it only lasted three days. Barbara was ordered out of Washington because federal forces were moving in again to threaten the district and because she was needed in the New York area.

The day after she left I was informed she was in a unit that had come under federal fire on its way north. All had been killed. As I said, it was a very temporary upturn.

Major Jeremy broke the news to me personally. He told me to take a few days off, then walked a few blocks with me, praising Barbara and giving me words of sympathy and encouragement. Not a single word stuck with me after his initial announcement. I was numb. My ears and my head stopped working. I remembered nothing. We wound up in some bar, where he bought me a drink. He made some offer to me about special counseling, to which I said nothing. After awhile he patted me on the back and left. There was still a war going on, and no one got special treatment.

Believe me, I know how Gil felt.

My weapon seemed heavy now. That's what I remember.

The Revolutionist

walking along, weapon slung over my shoulder, watching the hustle and bustle as our side prepared to defend the city against the federal troops closing in. That's when I had the idea. Federal troops closing in...I'd get the bastards. I would attack them. Me, James Lamberti, would make sure many of them wouldn't return to their loved ones either. I would avenge!

Quietly, nonchalantly, I asked a passing officer where the federals were coming in. Where was their closest penetration? He looked at me strangely a moment, then silently pointed northwest, up Wisconsin Avenue toward Bethesda. I started walking.

Well over an hour later I could hear shots. This was not the constant *rat tat tat* and *boom* of a full-fledged battle, rather the occasional sniper and defensive fire of two opposing forces as they first touched. There were no large-scale movements on either side yet. This suited my purposes perfectly. Swinging my weapon off my shoulder, I checked to make sure my magazine was full. On the way I had also "acquired" a grenade taken from the unattended side of an armored personnel carrier I'd passed. Advancing a few dozen more yards, I came up behind two of our troops huddled down behind a burned-out car. As I did, a shot from the government side whizzed by me.

One of the troops I approached glanced backward. Spotting me for the first time, he shouted, "Get down, you damn fool!"

I smiled, but continued walking toward them. Three or four more shots hit the car that protected them. The soldier who had shouted at me now took a few steps back, grabbed me and pulled me down.

"What the hell is wrong with you, buddy? You got a death wish?"

Looking directly at him, I replied, "Yeah, for them."

Then I jumped up, raced around him and the car and ran out into the pockmarked, cratered street in front of them. Lowering my weapon, I began firing wildly in the direction I'd seen the federal fire come from. I zigzagged as I advanced, dodging bullets that flew all around me.

Kill them! Kill the devils that took her away from me! It was the only thought in my mind.

Then something was wrong, and I was down. I couldn't move my left leg. Trying to rise again, I went down again. My head flipped down toward my feet. There was blood, a lot of it, pouring out of my leg. At first I was mad...no, furious that I'd been stopped. Then my stomach turned over. I heaved and felt very weak, and everything went black.

Chapter Eleven - N.Y.

"Okay everyone - prep. Over the top in ten minutes."

Word was passed up and down the line.

Over the top in ten minutes? I almost laughed. This sounded like we were in the trenches in World War I. All that was lacking was the command, "synchronize watches to...." Then I caught myself. There was nothing to laugh at here. Flipping my head first one way, then the next, I looked at all the people, the humanity, on both sides of me. They knew. Within an hour most of them, even if we were successful, would be dead. The sacrifice made by these people was truly above and beyond. And it was a willing sacrifice. They were losing their lives and their futures so that others could know freedom.

Tears streamed down my face as I thought of my two children. "Rachael, Sam...I love you so much. Know freedom, my children. Please, know freedom and have a good life! We here give this gift to you, if only you will seize it."

I started ramming my weapon's butt into the ground, hard, again and again. Suddenly, I felt a hand on my shoulder.

"Hey, buddy, I mean Captain Lamberti, sir. Are you all right?"

I looked up into the face of Gil, so young and yet so old.

"Oh, sorry, Gil. I was just...."

"Yeah, I know." He hunkered down beside me. "We're all dealing with something. I saw...you know, that you were having a little...whatever. So I checked everyone out for you, Captain. We're all ready, no matter what."

"Damn, Gil," I gulped. "You're getting a field promotion, right here and right now. You are now Sergeant Gil. We will make that official as soon as we get back."

"Thank you, sir!" Gil stood and saluted me, then laughed.

"That's not any crap, Mr. Gil. You are now a sergeant." Looking up at him, I knew what I felt. It was like being his father. Damn, he'd better live. If we both made it through this, he would have

122

a family again: mine.

Time to do my job. I shook my head and cleared my throat. "Gentlemen, final prep. Check your weapons. Remember the objective. Upon that objective everything depends. And good luck. May God be with you!"

My damn left leg was on fire again. I wanted another pain pill, but there weren't any. Taking a deep breath, I looked down at my leg. "Work, damn you, work - or else."

All down the line, tiny red lights flashed on.

*

"You with us, soldier?"

The voice was distant and dreamlike.

"Hey, are you with us?" It was gentle, like a feminine voice.

"Laura, I think he needs more blood. He's lost a lot."

Staring up toward the voice, my eyes slowly focused on a woman, a very pretty, blonde woman.

"Well, look at that. Mr. Lamberti is waking up." She smiled down at me gently.

"I was...I was. The last I remember...." I was still largely out of it, and the pain was hitting.

She was still smiling. "Yeah, we all know what you were doing. You were taking on the whole federal army yourself. It took eight other guys laying down a heavy blanket of fire to go out and get you. One of those guys took a bullet himself, but he'll be okay. You owe them, Sergeant Lamberti."

Thinking a second, I mumbled, "Yes, I do. As soon as I can get up."

"Well, that will be a while. The bullet you took in your leg nicked your main artery. You almost bled out, sergeant. Lucky for you I was there and dressed your wound on the spot. I managed to stop the bleeding; well, most of it. You know, another inch or two and you'd never have any more children. In fact, it was so close to 'intimate parts' that I think we have to get married."

The Revolutionist

The pretty lady smiled. Then, inexplicably, she looked up, her face turned gray and sullen, and she rose and walked off.

Now I was confused. I mumbled something as she walked away. The other woman came over to my side, gave me a quick, shallow grin, then watched the first woman as she left.

"What happened?" My weak voice croaked out. "Did I say something wrong?"

"No, sergeant. Ahh, Jackie, that's her name, she just lost her boyfriend a couple of weeks ago as we took Washington. Obviously she is...a little sensitive herself still. Anyway, I'm Laura, head nurse here and, as soon as you can get up, you go find her. You wouldn't be alive if she hadn't stopped the bleeding." Now Laura squeezed my hand, smiled and left.

Jackie, huh? Okay, I thought, I'll find you and thank you; as soon as I can.

It was four days before I could even sit, and another two days before I could slowly and carefully hobble. But hobble I did to find her. It was important to me to explain why I "went a little off" back there. Also, I wanted to ask her about her tragedy. As it turned out, everyone knew Jackie; she was a legend. The story was well known by everyone. Jackie had insisted on remaining by her boyfriend's side as we battled our way into Washington. It wasn't official, of course. She was supposed to remain behind with the Nursing Corps, but she wouldn't do it. The two of them practically led the charge into the city.

Fate always has its way. The battle was almost over. Most of the shooting had stopped, when her boyfriend, Captain Ed, rose from behind a row of bushes to signal the final march in. He was shot through the head and died instantly. The shots came from some government office building a block away. The story was that Jackie picked up his weapon, kissed him, then ran for the building. She made it. When the rest of the unit finally caught up with her, they found six dead federal troops. They also found her calmly sitting on a chair beside the bodies, smoking a cigarette.

DeEarlon

That night, as our troops stormed the Capitol and the White House, Jackie led the charge into the White House, where she killed the last four presidential guards. I've thought about Jackie and Barbara many times over the many months since we left Washington, and I snicker. Trust me, my friends, there's no contest about which sex is the deadliest. When a woman is angry, not even God can save you.

The loss of Washington to the feds had been put off for another two weeks on account of large contingents of federal government-hating segments of the Kentucky and Indiana National Guards arriving behind federal lines. They attacked the government troops from the rear without warning.

The feds had to go back to regroup and reinforce. That gave Jackie and me some time to talk, commiserate and soothe each other. Everyone who knew us assumed we were soothing each other completely, but nothing could have been further from the truth. It was too soon. The memory and warmth of those we'd loved and lost were still too close. What we did exchange were heartfelt memories and agonies. These were closer than any physical exchanges ever could have been.

Three days before we had to withdraw from the city, Jackie was given separate orders.

We talked before she left. She couldn't disclose her orders, only to say that we would almost certainly never meet again. It was then, for the first and only time, that we kissed.

Later on, walking back to my unit, I looked heavenward to Barbara and apologized, but I think she understood.

Massive federal forces were moving in around D.C. again. We were able to fight our way out solely because of those National Guard troops who came to our aid from the Midwest. They made all the difference for us but, nationally, rebel forces were having mixed results at best.

In the Northeast, initially at least, sympathy for us wasn't widespread. Far too many still believed the big-government lies

125

and their socialistic direction. The West Coast wasn't far behind in both aspects. We found the strongest support in the South and Midwest, where self-reliance and high morality still counted with most people.

As I've said, this really wasn't a regional division. It was a social and political issue. You either believed in big, all-controlling government or in freedom, individual effort and opportunity. There were few in between. That's why we were all amazed when we were almost pincered in between the feds who finally took D.C. back, and another fed army that surprised us from the south.

Someone came to our rescue again. A makeshift militia, calling itself The Minute Men, from New England, hit the feds from the D.C. area again. That allowed our army to escape to Ohio, where we had great local support.

The Minute Men fought furiously and sustained massive casualties in their effort. They intended to rush back to the Northeast to help our army there, but they'd been torn apart. What was left of them joined with us permanently. Their commander, General Silva from Rhode Island, mourned their losses, but made it very plain they all knew the dangers, and were proud and honored to have fought for freedom regardless of the cost.

For a few months there was a lull in large-scale hostilities. The only real shooting battles took place on the West Coast and consisted, for the most part, of small, running raids of one side against the other. We weren't deceived. During this lull, the feds were building three massive armies to move in and eventually crush us. They also launched 24/7 media campaigns to vilify us and build themselves into heroes. We did the best we could to get our own public relations campaign rolling, but when the other side is so massive, rich and media-controlling, it was almost impossible.

I was truly impressed with the intelligence of the average

citizen now. While they gave lip service to the feds, most supported us.

We knew that because whenever we were in the area, they gave us anything and everything we needed if they had it. That drove big government crazy. That craziness was shown when they would retaliate against whole areas for giving us help and support. The retaliation was often brutal. That completely destroyed their heroic image.

Still, they had the power.

Several foreign nations stepped up and volunteered to negotiate a peace. Of course these nations, to their credit, just wanted to stop the bloodshed. They had no intention of taking sides. We were reluctant to take part in such talks because a peace in place would leave the socialists in power, and getting the socialists out was the whole purpose of our rebellion. Because of our refusal to join any formal peace talks, we were held up around the world as not only the instigators of the bloodshed, but the continuing villains. Things turned very bad for us both nationally and internationally.

But G.W.I.M.W. (God Works In Mysterious Ways)

A small storekeeper in New York City got tired of all the government controls during the "unfortunate national conflict," as the federally-controlled media called it. He and a small number of friends marched on City Hall to complain. They were not allowed into the building, so they started shouting and chanting out in the street. The federal governor of New York City, a temporary position for wartime, came out and ordered them to be silent and to get off the street. The storekeeper, now completely indignant, shouted back that war or not, they had the right to speak.

We'll never know why, but after a second or two of fuming and puffing, the federal governor took out his sidearm and shot the storekeeper. Several people with the storekeeper rushed the governor, and he shot them too.

The Revolutionist

No, the federally-controlled media did not report the incident, but several dozen private cell phone cameras did. It was all over the nation within minutes, far too fast for the feds to stop the transmissions.

The storekeeper's name was Hector Ramirez, an immigrant who had come here from Guatemala for peace and opportunity. The incident began turning millions of Hispanic people, until now evenly split in this war, against the central government in Washington. An arrest warrant was immediately issued for the governor. Knowing he'd be thrown to the wolves in this situation, the governor disappeared. That only made matters worse. People thought the feds were hiding him. Riots and army desertions swept the country; and all this just before Washington was about to lower the boom on our rebel forces.

G.W.I.M.W. indeed.

American Freedom Fighters got yet another chance.

Over the next year the conflict became all-out war. We did well under General Ordway in the central Midwest. Our area of control was Ohio to Missouri, and down to Tennessee. We also controlled the Southeast from Georgia to Texas. The Northeast, however, was a different story. Though the people there were increasingly anti-federal, the government's stranglehold was strong. Except for New Hampshire and Maine, those that would rebel had nothing to rebel with. The government had seized their weapons long ago.

On the West Coast, Washington state was relatively quiet and both sides wondered at this. But just outside Portland, Oregon, we rebels won a massive battle that almost destroyed all federal forces in the area.

Most of California remained in flux. Enormous federal forces there were met with some of our best hit-and-run troops as well as large, mob-type armies not truly under our control. They were freelance, libertarian crowds that many said didn't even feel bullets when they hit. Though not strongly allied with us, they truly hated the feds.

The Colorado story was another tragedy that became known everywhere. The Air Force Academy had always leaned toward supporting the rebels. Once that became clear and their planes represented a threat to the government, Washington didn't hesitate. The people around Colorado Springs swore that it was an atomic bomb, but in truth it wasn't. Twenty or more large missiles all with the largest conventional explosive warheads, struck in unison. They did produce a mushroom cloud, and the ground shook up to forty miles away, but there were no nukes. Where the academy had been there now existed an enormous crater.

And so it went for more than a year. I took part in several small battles that kept the feds out of our controlled area. The feds, for their part, started moving most of their forces south of Washington, through Virginia and toward the Carolinas. To accomplish this, they pulled most of their troops out of the Northeast, where they felt very secure. They would regret that move.

*

"Get ready, any second now." I'd pulled my men up in preparation for the assault. Before this I'd talked to each one personally, feeling them out. Central command had picked well. These were tough men, but at the same time very human. I'll never forget what one man said to me. His name was Boris, and he was second-generation American, parents from Russia.

It went like this, "Are you set. Boris? Are you completely prepared for this?"

"Yes, and no."

"What does that mean?"

"It means I'm sad to be here."

" Sad? Are you afraid? Do you want to stay here?"

"Oh no. What I mean is, I shouldn't have to be here. This

whole situation shouldn't exist here, not in America. My parents came here for freedom and personal opportunity, as I'm sure your people came here also. They didn't come here for this socialist bullshit. For that, they could have stayed in Russia. What happened? What happened to the voters to pick such bad people? Was it the drugs, a cushy life style, bad education?

"I'm sorry I have to be here, but I'm not sorry that I can still fight for what America used to be." He turned away and stared out over the killing field in front of him.

Gil was behind me. Neither one of us said anything.

Back to waiting for that final signal.

Chapter Twelve - N.C.

They were safe. Thank you, God! I felt my eyes tearing up. A runner had just handed me a message that got through from Canada. Barbara's parents sent a message that Rachael and Sam were safe and well. They all missed Barbara terribly and always would, but they wanted me to know my children were okay. I always knew my in-laws were good, strong people. How was it possible this got through? Don't know, don't care!

I folded the slip of paper the message was written on very tightly, at least eight times. Slipping it into a breast pocket, I buttoned the pocket, then patted the outside of the pocket three times. I pressed my hand there the third time for long seconds. Somehow, it was like keeping my children close to me and safe. But we had a job to do.

In our arrogance, we'd thought some of our areas were completely protected. What's the old saying about never assuming anything? We assumed Atlanta was safe. It was deep within territory we held. We were wrong. In an amazing maneuver by federal forces, they captured the city; just the city, deep behind our lines. They accomplished this by using procedures not commonly used today. They did a massive paratroop drop, at night, over the city itself. That's very dangerous for the troops being dropped. If you get hung up on a tall building, you're either target practice for the other side, or you wait for your lines to break and down you go.

We saw the planes coming in on our radar, but what we expected was bombing. What we got were enemy troops. By dawn, they had over 5,000 troops in downtown Atlanta. We had virtually none. We didn't need troops in a city deep within our own lines, or so we thought. Yet a second surprise awaited us. Twenty miles north of Atlanta, a federal army of over 20,000 more had somehow clandestinely penetrated our lines. None of this was meant to attack us from the rear, it was meant to take Atlanta - period. They wanted to say they had captured a major prize and struck a severe blow to those "traitorous rebels."

It was a severe blow. General Ordway was wild. He blamed his subordinates, of course, but his worst furry was reserved for himself. How had he missed this? He prided himself on always thinking "outside the box." He was always ten moves ahead on the chess board.

No one dared get near him. All available troops were called up, to whit, I was packing my duffle. We expected to hit them hard and all at once. Everyone expected that. Of course, everyone was wrong.

Ordway went into semi-seclusion for 48 hours. We thought he had a nervous breakdown. But no: He was brainstorming. He was legendary for the completely unique maneuver, and that's what he came up with. There would be no massive assault on Atlanta to take it back. Only one unit would go in, the First Freedom Fighters; my unit.

Ordway reasoned it this way: There were roughly 150,000 federal troops in New England. Washington thought this area fairly safe for the feds, so they withdrew 80 to 90 percent of those troops. Why and where? They were only using 25,000 to attack and secure the Atlanta area. What were they going to do with the other 120,000 or so?

Obviously, Ordway thought, the feds were going to throw that huge force against the back of our Freedom Fighters as we tried to retake the city. Oh no they wouldn't! Ordway would have our full Freedom Fighter Force set a trap for the larger federal force. Our full forces, that is, except the First Freedom Fighter unit, would retake Atlanta alone. Yeah, all 9,000 of us. I was reeling. Ordway had a lot of faith in our unit. I hoped we had a lot of miracle in us.

The First, as we called ourselves, was summoned to a special assembly with "the old man." Immediately we were presented with the latest taped speech by Athenson, reminding us that we had to save the nation not only for our good, but so the nation could continue to save the world. A lot of us looked down at that statement. We were tired. But Athenson continued, mentioning something I'd almost forgotten. It was a quote from Thomas Jefferson; something about "the tree of liberty having to be watered by blood every few years." It was being well watered now.

After the recording, Ordway told us we would be able to cope with the much larger force, already in Atlanta, for two reasons. First, they would be softened up for us before we attacked, and second, we were the First, the best, and we were fighting for the freedom of our nation. Most of the guys still cheered at this, though maybe not quite as loudly as before. Someone asked him about this "softening up," and intensive bombing killing a lot of noncombatants as well as fed troops. Was that right?

Ordway said there would be no bombing. They had other "softening" methods. He gave no explanation. We went to immediate prep for attack.

During that night many of our planes and a lot of drones flew overhead. Something was happening in the city. Through the darkness we could see a misty smoke rising, but no loud bangs and no fire. Just before dawn, as we prepared to move in, everyone had it figured out. A gas of some sort was being dropped, and it couldn't be lethal or the civilians would die too.

As we moved in, our superior officers informed us of the gas. It was a specially-formulated sickening gas. It was truly nauseating, causing the worst flu-like symptoms you've ever had. It dissipated after only six hours, so we should be fine, but the effects on those who breathed it lasted for at least 12 hours. Be quick and be careful, we were told. Many, they were sure, would still be in fighting condition.

So we moved in to retake Atlanta. It proved a much tougher job than any of us had anticipated. This was not classic warfare.

The Revolutionist

This was bloody, block to block street fighting, and the feds held the high ground. Virtually every high-rise building had teams of shooters in it; from six stories up and on every side. Yes, they had been affected by the gas and almost half were down and squirming in heavy nausea all around us. Those we gathered up quickly and marched away, when they could walk. The problem was that almost half had somehow escaped the full effects of the gas and that was still enough to make our efforts pure hell - and to kill or wound close to 2,000 of us. It was 24 hours before the city was ours again, and the cost was high, but we were lucky.

The trap that General Ordway had set for the government army had sprung just as Ordway planned. Our main force completely surprised them, and won. They, however, surprised us with some new, powerful hand grenades and a fighting spirit we didn't expect. We won the battle, but its effect on our war effort was near catastrophic.

Our "victory" cost us over 25,000 killed or wounded out of a total committed force of just over 50,000. It was worse for the other side. Of the 120,000 they sent in, only 40,000 lived, and they ran for their lives. Here's where the true horror of war comes in. The phrase "bloodbath" comes to mind. We could not afford any prisoners. We had no means of guarding that many, or feeding them, or taking care of them. It was ordered that we take no prisoners. No one in the main force felt good about that, but it really was a simple decision; their life or yours. And you wonder why so many soldiers come back from war with more wounds in their heads than in their bodies.

It was without a doubt the bloodiest battle ever to take place on American soil. Neither side would do any bragging about this battle.

The government in Washington experienced another defeat as a result. They had felt very secure about the Northeast, withdrawing most of their troops there. It was an area that contained the most socialist sympathizers, after all. Even socialists, however, have limits when they're starving and freezing.

Most of the food in the Northeast came in from other areas of the country. These areas, the food-producing ones, were either under rebel control, or the rebels could block food distribution to the region. Fuel for the Northeast mimicked the food situation; it came from elsewhere or was blocked. As if that weren't bad enough, the socialist government in Washington truly showed its sparkling stupidity by blocking, per environmental department order, the burning of wood. War or not, burning wood was, in their opinion, an environmental disaster for the Earth.

Disaster is an interesting word. They didn't seem to know or care that, without wood burning, the Northeast couldn't heat homes or cook what little food was available. Cases of people being arrested for just burning candles for a little light were even highlighted and bragged about. All this even though electricity was strictly rationed as well.

As I think back, this was pure stupidity. But in their leaders' limited, socialist minds this was a good thing. They were sure that good socialists would suffer and sacrifice for their noble, common cause. First you obey their good socialist law, then you save the environment.

Meanwhile people froze to death and starved in the dark. Many died. Their policies made good sense, especially since so many of those people were their loyal followers.

The riots began three days after the Battle of Atlanta, and Washington was both unprepared and shocked. Riots went on for over a week until they could move more troops into the Northeast from other areas. Those troops stopped the rioting - cold! In every city and town, troops dragged people - often completely innocent people - out into the street and shot them in public as examples. It had an effect. Many of those loyal socialists came over to the rebel side, and a guerrilla war begun behind federal lines. Good job, Washington, as usual.

As we were securing Atlanta, I met an old friend, Colonel

The Revolutionist

Derman, specialist in covert action. We hadn't seen each other since my initial training outside Richmond. The colonel was brought back to the Atlanta area to assess prospects of further infiltration by federal spies. He brought me up to date on events on the West Coast, where he had been active for over a year.

He told me that in Washington state, where things had been fairly quiet, the government in D.C. had secretly smuggled federal troops in through British Columbia, Canada, and down into the state to solidify their power there. The secret got out, and Canadian authorities "went ballistic." They actually threatened military action if the troops were not withdrawn. They also wanted a public, international apology for the violation of Canadian sovereignty.

There was an apology, sort of public, but the feds didn't withdraw their troops. Our men, the Freedom Fighters, had a large contingent in Idaho, next door. They immediately attacked the federal troops and virtually wiped them out. Washington state was now, for all intents and purposes, in the rebel camp. Most of Oregon was already ours.

Now, on to California. There were three forces at play here. The feds had two large armies moving up and down the Pacific Coast, and we had two large armies opposing them. There was, however, a third player. Latin American gangs had united into a fairly large force themselves. They wanted a separate Hispanic nation, as in that secret plan we'd discovered a couple of years before. The bottom line was: California was a mess. It was pure chaos.

I thanked Derman for the update and invited him to a special dinner we were preparing. It was a sort of victory dinner, at least for the Atlanta area.

"Can't do it, Jim. I just finished my investigation of this area and I have to move on at once. You're clear of feds here, but they're regrouping elsewhere. They want a final, complete victory nationwide. They're going to pull out all the big guns."

DeEarlon

"What are we going to do in response, colonel? This "victory" cost us. We're pretty tired now."

"We're also regrouping, Jim. You'll get new marching orders any day now. Good luck, captain. Oh, and I'm sorry, truly sorry. I heard about Barbara. She was a great woman, Jim." We saluted and shook hands. He clasped my shoulder before turning away. I always liked Derman. I haven't seen him since.

The events swirling around the Battle of Atlanta changed everything. The rebels pretty much secured the Northwest, we re-secured the Southeast, the Midwest grew stronger for us, and we left California for now to run its own mess.

The biggest change was in the Northeast. New England and New York state were no longer dependable for Washington. That was good for us. Within two weeks, somehow, we started getting a few volunteers from the Northeast. We had no idea how some of them got through federal lines, so none got vital jobs. What they did accomplish, however, was freeing up many trusted troops for more important assignments.

It's a good thing, too, because Derman wasn't wrong about the feds pulling out the big guns.

*

I shifted my position, waiting. Damn, my neck, back and legs told me I wasn't young anymore. Snickering to myself, I thought of more battle humor. Don't worry, Jim, you may not get any older.

Tension was high. We all knew this was the decisive day. If we lost this desperate struggle, the war might go on for another few weeks, but we would definitely lose. Upon the next few hours, everything rested.

So you think. That's all you can do. Was it all worth it, all the deaths and all the suffering and destruction? I guess it depends on the people. The people really do make their own country. You can sit back and do as you're told. Have every aspect of your life

137

run by the government and delight in the scraps they throw to you. Then you are peasants.

Or you can demand to rule your own life, full of freedom and opportunity. You can throw the buzzards out of office who would rule you, and only pick politicians who will protect your ability to rule your own life.

First, though, you must know! You must know the difference between the politicians, and that takes study. That's your job as a citizen - to study and to know. Pick the ones who will protect your ability to rule your own life. So many don't know, or are too lazy. But there is worse: Many don't care.

As in ancient Rome, all many people care about is bread and circus. The nation, the great republic, dissolves as some seize all power and wealth and throw bread and circus at the people - the peasants, really. At that point, you are a peasant. And you deserve to be one.

Not those here, though. They are fighting for freedom as so many have before. My eyes drift over to Boris, sitting, waiting. He knows the price. We all know the price; blood and war. We choose freedom, and there will always be those who will.

Shame on those who don't understand that you can't wait until they have taken most of your rights. Then it's too late. You must raise your voice and vote in protest the first time they cross the line and clip your rights and freedoms. You must pay attention and challenge them locally, statewide or nationally. If you don't, this is where the road leads.

Was that the signal?

*

It was about a month after Derman left that we saw what he meant. Washington wasn't wasting any more troops. They held back their forces to protect the territories they controlled and keep the people in those areas strictly under their thumb. Most battles, at least on their side, were now being fought with drones, missiles, robots and any high-tech products they controlled; and they controlled a lot.

Immediately after Atlanta, we had the momentum. That was to shift within ninety days. A massive, mostly technological invasion of the Northwest restored federal rule there. They took no prisoners this time. Again, though, people are strange. The citizens of the Northwest, formerly rather quiet, now began a guerrilla campaign against the feds, just as in the Northeast. Give people a taste of freedom as compared with iron rule and.... Well, you know.

California and the Midwest were both left alone for now. Washington concentrated on the South next, and we were in the South. Initially they attacked us with technology more than troops, just as they'd done in the Northwest. It worked. We were devastated. General Ordway called in all our reserves. He made a decision. We would make a last, massive attack on the nation's capital again. If we could capture it a second time, and hold it, we might have a chance for success, or at the very least, a strong negotiating position.

The First Freedom Fighters made a lightning strike from the northern border of Georgia, across the Carolinas, largely ours, to the southern border of Virginia. There we hit strong opposition. With some brilliant maneuvers by General Ordway, we managed to fight our way up to central Virginia. Now Washington was in sight.

Just as importantly, Ordway's psychological analysis of the arrogant, self-aggrandizing buzzards in Washington was correct. They would not take us out with bombs, poison gas or anything technological. They wanted us alive. The man who disgracefully occupied the oval office could accept nothing less. He wanted to march us through the streets of Washington and hang us in public as we had hung the bloody, corrupt leaders before.

We fought our way to the outskirts of Charlottesville, Virginia, less than 100 miles from the capital. It was there that they threw everything they had at us. Our army took shelter behind a natural berm there, and what wasn't natural, we built ourselves.

So here we've been for over a month, slowly being whittled down. It's become evident we'll never move any closer to Washington. The feds have assembled a massive force in front of us. This time they withdrew forces from New Jersey and Pennsylvania to bolster their army around Washington. Oh, and wouldn't you know it, both New Jersey and Pennsylvania have erupted in rioting and night warfare against their federal rulers, so loved are they.

Waiting here, it has occurred to me this is the height of irony in one respect. We sit here, rebels, fighting in central Virginia against a federal government that we regard as way out of control. A little less than 200 years ago, this is exactly where federal and rebel forces clashed in the last civil war. That conflict didn't end too well for the rebels.

But this was a war of a different persuasion. This was a war for freedom. On second thought, maybe it wasn't such a different war after all.

*

The signal? It was! The first prep signal was given. On the next our main force moves out. My unit waits until the actual engagement of forces on each side so a small valley of least resistance can be opened for us and our special mission.

I'm prepped, tensed and ready to go, as are all my men. My vision is now concentrated across the top of the stump, and something catches my eye.

A column of ants is marching from one side of the stump into a hole on the other side. They carry some sort of food for the colony. They care not for our world. They have their own. They will not stop their work regardless of our actions. Even if they are crushed, they will carry on.

An omen, perhaps?

DeEarlon

Chapter Thirteen - R.I.

There's an explosion of men and movement all around me as the final signal is given. A few initial shots are fired from the government side as our troops, our main force, crest the berm. It's amazingly good luck. They haven't caught on to the reality of the situation yet: a full-scale rebel assault. Every second of government delay is a mini-victory for us. More shots. Our main force has almost gained their line. Are they that distracted by their own prep? Is it possible?

Almost there.

The thunder is deafening. More than half our advancing force goes down. As in the past, a flash of old films from the trench warfare of World War I goes through my mind. I convulse and stop breathing, but I hold the puke down. Still our unit awaits the special signal meant just for us.

It seems hours. Our assault force, or what's left, gains the government line. We all know well the pure hell, fury and death that's taking place only a few hundred yards in front of us. Suddenly there are explosions everywhere behind the federal lines. That's planned. It's part of the "opening" process. The plan calls for a second round of explosions about 50 yards behind the first. That will be our signal to go.

The explosions come, and my unit, made up of brave, experienced fighters, hesitates. It's pure death out there, and they know it.

Clearing the top of the berm, I stand, straight and tall, and yell to them, "Come on, guys, half a mile to victory! *Half a mile!*" I wave my weapon forward, high through the air. First two, then five, then ten, then all, they finally crest the berm. We run low and fast, with bullets whistling past us everywhere.

You try not to think as you race toward the hell you know awaits. The mission, that's it; that's all you think of. Thinking of anything else weakens and slows you. And that kills you.

It was a miracle - truly! Shots and explosions can be heard everywhere, but not one shot at us as we cross the pockmarked field. Our main force has taken the blow and driven the enemy back. Good job, guys, and then we find the price they've paid.

Within 10 yards of where the federal line had been, the ground is covered with bodies - our bodies. Not all are dead. Some still moan and twist, but we can't stop or it will all be in vain. Soon we're jumping over federal bodies. We're not as careful not to step on them.

Racing, racing; now we're taking fire. A man to my left is hit and down. Then, from the corner of my eye, I see two more of our unit go down to heavy automatic fire from the far right. Almost instinctively, Gil, three more in the unit, and I turn our weapons to where we think the fire is coming from. It continues, however, until I see an explosion. Someone from our unit is close enough to use a grenade.

We race on again. It should be less then half a mile now to our objective, the helicopter landing site. But it's only another couple hundred yards until we catch up with our own front line, stopped cold.

Oh, God help us! Our assault force hasn't opened the way for us. They're pinned down before a solid wall of resistance, one we hadn't expected or planned for!

I signal my troops to stay low. As soon as we appear in the middle of the battle, we start taking fire. Several men crawl over to me.

"Can't get bogged down here, sir! We'll never make it." The words of a young, exuberant soldier.

"I have a stupid question." It was Boris. "Did the chopper even come in? I never saw it. No chopper, no purpose."

It was a fair, and dangerous question. This whole operation exists for the contents of that helicopter. Had it even arrived? My ears perked up and my eyes shifted skyward.

The Revolutionist

"Oh yeah. It arrived." I pointed upward for the whole unit to see. Two laser beams crisscrossed back and forth way up in the air.

"They're holding it down for us, guys. We'd better damn well make it. Let's not disappoint 'em!"

"Then let's go." A young, gung-ho soldier jumps up and runs forward, too high, too brave and too close. Before I can signal him down again, he's hit by multiple shots. His body is picked up and thrown backward. No one else moves.

Looking forward, I see someone else scurrying toward me from the regular troops in the front line. I expect him to tell me that the main force is pulling back. I turn out to be wrong.

"Sir, sir; are you the special ops team?"

"We are, sergeant. What's up?"

"Just received a radio message. Lay low until further contact, and we're to fall back slightly."

"So we're getting out? This is the end?"

"No, sir. You won't believe this. We surprised the feds as they were prepping their tanks a while back. We've captured most of the tanks and we destroyed most of the rest. But even better, sir. Remember last year when Washington ordered the Air Force Academy wiped out because they didn't trust them? Well, the flyboys didn't forget. Many of their friends were in Colorado Springs when it was wiped off the map, and many of them had been trained there themselves. Well, sir, it's payback time! We're laying low because we've got some heavy air support coming in. While we're waiting, tank fire is going to open that corridor for both of us. Then, when the jets leave, the tanks will accompany us right up to 'Chopper Field,' sir."

All this took a few seconds to sink in. Then I had a few questions. "Where did you get a radio, sergeant? I thought the feds blocked or tapped our frequencies long ago."

"They did, sir. But a few of us were issued them last night because...well, this is a last effort, sir, so they figured, what the hell...ya know..."

"Got it, sergeant. Maybe you don't know, but why don't these incoming aircraft just take out that magic chopper?"

"Actually sir, I do know because I asked command the same question. They don't want those traitors dead. They're of no value then. They want them alive, just like the feds want us alive, well, most of us. They have real value then, and we can do some old-fashioned horse trading."

I smile at that. It actually makes sense. "All right, sergeant, we don't move."

Only seconds after those words, air-to-ground missiles come screaming in far ahead of us, followed by 70mm cannon fire from the planes. This "last generation" of manned jets is the epitome of an air weapon, and they're protected by the new electronic shields that make them almost impossible to take out. The area directly in front of our troops erupts as though thousands of pounds of explosives are setting off underground. Their attack only lasts six minutes, but that's all that's needed. How ironic that in the government wiping out so many of the pilots' comrades, it manages to enrage and turn the rest.

The way opens at last. I look skyward and thank the "Man Upstairs." I know we would never have made it on our own. There were just too many feds and they were too heavily armed.

A minute or so after the sky boys roar away, our captured tanks mov in, clearing the way, and we need those tanks over the next few hundred yards.

No one had anticipated just how large the government army is. We have a new ally though: confusion. Those in Washington or in the federal command here never anticipated what just happened any more than we had. The government troops are still in shock and not steady on their feet. Many pull back or scatter.

I give the order for my men to advance. We might never have this chance again. We move fairly easily through the next 300-400 yards, before that damned government numerical advantage hits us again. I can see them now, the two large boulders that mark the western end of the field the presidential helicopter has settled in. We're almost there.

Gil takes point with me. We rush ahead and shout back to the rest of our special outfit. If I could grab Gil, I'd shake that hell out of him, the dumb kid. I know he wants revenge for his family, and he can almost taste it now. But he's pulling ahead of me, blasting away on both sides as he runs, getting to within five yards of the feds.

I rise straight up and scream at him, not that he can hear me in the din of battle, but I have to try. I have to. Suddenly a searing pain tears through my left side. It stops me for a second, and in that second another pain tears through my right calf. I collapse. Unable to move for what seems like an eternity, I finally raise my head. As I do, I see Gil's body rise and be thrown backward, then disappear. It all takes place in slow motion, or seems to. My breathing freezes. My mind screams, "No, God! *No!*" But my lips never move.

Now, somehow, I force myself up, waving my men forward. Forward, forward, we must go! Fire is heavy now: it almost fills the air. Look, look for Gil, I tell myself, eyes sweeping the ground. Where, where? Then a crumpled lump appears on the muddy ground. I fall to my knees next to it. It's Gil. His mouth is open and his blank eyes stare skyward. I choke, then I close his eyelids and push his mouth shut.

"Damn kid, damn kid.... Damn kid!" No tears can come from me. Only deep, hard breaths. Slamming my weapon's butt into the ground, I scream, "No! This isn't fair, damn it!"

Then I mutter something like, "Go to your family now, Gil. Go and embrace...forever."

Several bullets hit the ground in front of me, and my mind goes blank. My head snaps up and I see Boris taking point as our team reaches some boulders. I try to stand, but my right leg won't work. Pushing with my left leg, holding my right steady, I finally rise. Sheer willpower forces me forward. James Lamberti will get the bastards, all of them. How dare you bastards rob our land not only of freedom, but of life? All the dreams and young lives: wasted. I blast away at any face I see now, for only the feds face my way.

The boulder. I reach the boulder. I fall against it. My vision sweeps the field beyond. Boris is beside me and most of the unit directly behind. I can see the helicopter far ahead. Its rotors are turning but it can't rise because of the laser beams above it. There must be a hundred feds in front of it, and the fire is as thick as fog.

We have to make it. We have to make those last few yards! Having trouble walking now, I shout to Boris to take them in. He looks at me questioningly for a moment, then sees my side and leg. He smiles and replies, "No problem, boss."

Raising his arm in a wave, Boris and the unit surge forward. I take a few deep breaths to recharge and keep the pain down. Then, I too step out, away from the boulder, attempting to follow. I raise my weapon.

*

As I remember it, it was like a gust of bright wind. That's the only way I can describe it. There was no pain, just a flash and great pressure. Then a sort of fog for awhile. As the fog began to clear, I had trouble focusing my eyes. My vision wasn't quite right and a strange silence enveloped me. There was movement all around me, but it was completely silent.

Had I lost my other ear drum? No, this was a different silence. Slowly, I tried to focus again and finally I looked down. Some poor fellow lay there on the ground near where I had been. His face and upper uniform were blown away. Still there was something familiar about him. I couldn't think of it just then.

*

The Revolutionist

Wait, what about the mission? I've had to catch up with my men. I try to look toward the chopper. Eyes. Damn, can't quite focus! It's foggy, sort of. There's the battle still going on in the distance. Boris racing forward, hand up, waving the men on.

No! Now Boris goes down. Who's that? It's Marv Taylor taking point. Looks like he's been shot in the head, a lot of blood running down his face. He's still moving though, urging the men on.

The team is actually at the chopper! One of our guys blasts the rotor. They can't take off now. I cheer inside. The side door of the aircraft slides opens, and heavy fire pours out. Then it suddenly ceases. Our men swarm around the door.

I want to be there. Trying to move forward, but I don't seem to make any progress. What's wrong with me?

Move your legs Lamberti! Move 'em!

Looking down now. Where are my legs? Have I gone crazy? Hey, I don't feel any pain in my right leg or my left side anymore. That's good, I guess. Wait a minute! My vision slowly goes back to that poor guy on the ground behind me. He has no face, but he does have a bloody hole in his left side and a clean shot through his right leg.

NO! That's...that's...ME! I'm laying on the ground. I'm dead. I'm dead. How can that happen? How can that be? How can I be looking at myself dead?

Get up, Jim. Get up and put your face back on! I'd shiver and cry, but I can't. I can't. Me, or whatever is me, freezes for a moment, not knowing what to do. I'm confused, confused but not frightened.

The battle still rages furiously in spots. Men going down everywhere, and it's hard to describe this to you, their "presences" rising as their hearts stop.

There's no difference between us now, the rebels and the feds, just a passing recognition and a tug of something they're leaving behind as their essence rises. There is a sadness, but a peculiar release.

That living world, I still have an interest. What's happening at the chopper? I'm going there. Not moving as in the life world, but still going. I don't know how, but eventually I'm there.

A group comes to the door, stiff, sullen, unhappy. My men, or former men, are pointing their weapons up at them; giving them orders. They are generals and, yes, yes, the president; the big prize. Accomplishment overwhelms my presence and I glow.

I sense a voice from way back in the helicopter. I can't hear it exactly, but I sense it. The captured government leaders are unhappy with it. Two of the leaders have fury on their faces. The president has fear, deep fear, in his soul. The unseen voice radiates again and one of the generals pulls a handgun from a breast pocket. He turns to fire back into the chopper's interior while pulling another government leader in front of him for cover. He never gets the shot off. He is shot from that unseen presence behind him first and tumbles out the chopper door.

My men rush to him. He's not dead, no presence rises from him. My men, my unit, secure him. I sense the presence from the chopper's far back giving more orders, loud and strong. The government men are enraged, except for the president, who is still terrified.

One of the generals, I believe on orders from the unseen presence, pulls out a small communicator. He talks into it, then hands it to the president, who, reluctantly, also talks into it, loudly and with many words. I have no sense of time as in the former world, but there's a feeling of less conflict after - after what? - I don't know.

A more peaceful sense of everything begins to settle around me. The government leaders are disembarking from the chopper now. Their hands are being tied. I have a strong sense of commands being made and emanating from the back of the helicopter again. The presence back there begins moving, coming forward. I focus my "sight" as it were, on the chopper

The Revolutionist

door.

The unseen presence appears. It's Jackie, my old friend! She is holding a MAC-12 machine pistol and barking orders strongly. My being understands now what her secret orders were. I switch my concentration to the president. He feels betrayed and ashamed. Ah, somehow I know Jackie was intimate with this man. She drained him of his secrets and now she has crushed him, him and his world. Her sense is now glowing; it's a sense of triumph and ultimate revenge.

Immediately my awareness of the area begins to change. There is less chaos and less danger.

Though I can't hear, there seem to be fewer violent vibrations through the thin fog that envelops me. Without a true sense of time, I don't know when the next thing happened, I can only relate it.

General Ordway comes into the scene. He's shaking hands and saluting. He speaks harshly to the government officers and even more harshly to the president. He goes to Jackie and salutes her with the greatest respect. Then he drops the salute, and hugs her warmly. He seems to say something about a nightmare ending. Another officer approaches. Major Jeremy from the training center is with him. Both officers point back behind them, back in the direction of my body. All are silent for a time, whatever time is now. Then all salute in my body's direction.

Jackie begins to shake and drops the machine pistol. She then drops to her knees, crying. I want to comfort her, hold her and tell her all is well, but I cannot. My presence tries to envelop her and tell her not to cry. It seems to get through somehow. She at least stops crying and rises. Many more soldiers now flood in. The prisoners are led away.

A new officer quickly strides up to General Ordway. He is a high-ranking officer, but I don't know him. Ordway salutes him too. Actually, they salute each other. There is a sense of relief, happiness. Ordway shakes his hand fiercely. I suddenly recognize

150

the uniform. He seems to be *the* ranking officer with government Special Forces. I get it now. Our rebel high command has been working secretly for over a year to turn our greatest government opponent, Special Forces, away from the feds and to our side. They turned. Like most of the Air Force, they turned.

Thank God!

There is a lot involved in a revolution. Hearts are just as important as guns. No, I'm wrong. Hearts are far more important than guns. Guns only do what the hearts tell them to do.

Another presence approaches me. It indicates that we must go. We pass to a new place. Do not fear, it tells me, this is far from the end.

*

Where am I? What time has passed, a minute, a year? There is no sense of time as I have known it. I'm comforted by the other presence, who seems to be my guide. We are in a city, no, yes - in some city. My guide is joyful. He indicates another presence is coming, one my essence will delight in. I feel the other presence. Then I "see" her. It's Barbara, and all my being soars. We "embrace," and I swear I can feel her next to me again. She indicates her immense joy and has much to "tell" me. First, she "senses" to me that she has "seen" the children and they are well, as are her parents. I glow even more. But both Barbara and the guide now "say" we are here, in this place, for another reason. After our visit here, we will go "home" and await all our loved ones there.

Barbara asks me if I recognize this place. I "look" and feel. Yes, I decide. This is Washington. We are somewhere in the capital. My guide indicates we are here for a good reason, one that will justify our existence and pain in our former world. The guide and Barbara sweep forward toward a large plaza. I'm swept along, still not totally sure how to move in my new form.

Looking down on the plaza, it's filled with people. Flags

are flying everywhere. There should be a din rising from this many people, but I have no hearing. Now Barbara and my guide indicate a sort of trick to me. They show me how to concentrate on the vibrations that flow through the air, and with the vibrations comes a certain level of "hearing." Not hearing as I've known it in life, but an understanding nevertheless. It's a happy revelation. My guide now indicates the podium in front of the crowd. We all concentrate.

The din from the crowd, now perceivable by me, begins to grow. I observe a small pod of individuals approaching the podium. The one at front center appears familiar to me. As he mounts the steps, I recognize him. It's Professor Athenson, and as he takes the podium, the crowd explodes in cheers. Is he of higher office now? Perhaps he is the president. He raises his hands to the deafening cheers of the throng.

"Ladies and gentlemen, I greet you as one free American to another." The thunder from the mass of people actually rattles the streetlight fixtures.

"The nation lives, still in one piece, but even more importantly, it lives in freedom!" The light fixtures rattle again from the thunderous applause.

"We are here today in joy that freedom has been restored to our nation. That those who would have robbed it from us have been torn down. That both the socialism and the oligarchy they would have imposed on us have been crushed. For now, and only for now, we have dodged the bullet of socialism; that system that seems so attractive to so many, but crushes the personal dreams and personal initiative of people, and eventually of nations.

Yes, yes, it is often more difficult following your own path, but it is what makes life worth living. But be not deceived, my fellow Americans. The fight is not over, it will never be over. Freedom is always bought and maintained at the cost of blood and struggle. Vigilance and blood are the eternal prices that will ever be paid for freedom. Remember this first: if you have a freedom and a right, don't let them take it from you. Once gone, it will never return. Scratch, kick, and fight bravely for every right.

Do not be afraid to sacrifice to keep your rights. The pain and suffering of the struggle to keep them will be nothing to the pain of their loss. Remember also, that pain and struggle *will* come again. You, your children, your children's children will be called on to step forward with courage again. Freedom, like breathing, requires constant effort. Witness what has just occurred and the cost of our victory. We must have the courage that they had. Who were they? Who are they? They are the ones who stood up, who spoke up, who stepped forward, and ultimately shed their blood for us...all of us. They would not allow the "kings" to rule.

They were not deceived by all the false promises and hollow gifts of these quislings. Those who fought for us said, the people must rule. We must never forget their sacrifice. We must honor them by not allowing any government excesses again - *never again!* We can and will rule our own lives."

More thunder from the crowd.

"If anyone running for office ever proposes anything that takes your personal freedom away or your right to rule your own property, deny them! If anyone running for office proposes any laws or rules beyond the absolute minimum, deny them! If anyone running for office proposes taxation or programs beyond the minimum necessary and sensible, deny them!

"In such denials, you honor those who laid down their lives for you. *Never, ever forget this*, or you deny their sacrifices, their memories and their very souls, as well as your own future."

Barbara and my guide huddle close to me at these words.

"When we leave here today, we will go to a new national cemetery, an enormous one. It will hold the thousands upon thousands who died in this horrendous national conflict. Each one gave up their freedom, their future, their very lives so that you - we - could have freedom, future and life, a free life of our own choosing without government interference.

"So many died, and we will honor each and every one. That is the right and just thing to do. But one has been picked for special honor. An ordinary person who merely wanted to live his life unencumbered. A husband and father, who wanted a good future for his family and a better life for his children. The government, however, was crushing him; him and his dreams and his family's dreams, so he took up arms, a drastic step, but a last, desperate hope.

He was one of the first and certainly one of the bravest. He is a shining example of what free people and free nations are all about. If more people had shown his courage and devotion in the beginning, perhaps this horrible maelstrom could have been totally avoided.

"When his body was found, identification was nearly impossible, but we discovered his identity. Because of that, we were able not only to identify him, but learn his story. It is the true story of a man, a citizen, a human being who couldn't take it anymore. His beloved wife, Barbara, was also lost in the conflict. Both did extraordinary things, far above and beyond. Together with others, so many others, they stood up bravely for their rights and freedoms.

"Unfortunately, Barbara's body was never found, but I'm sure - out there - they are together again.

"All the headstones in our new national cemetery will be arranged in military formation, and his stone will stand at the front of the parade. We now know his full name, but, with his family's permission, we will not use it. Whenever he talked to someone, he always said, "Just call me Jim." And that is what will be on his headstone. It will read:

"Captain Jim, who led the charge - Thank You - you and your brave and beloved wife, Barbara."

"You are an eternal light and fighter for freedom, Captain Jim, and you will forever be known as the Revolutionist."

DeEarlon

It seemed the thunder from the crowd now rattled the very stones of the capital itself as tears rolled down the cheeks of the multitudes assembled. My guide gave me a sort of nudge, and Barbara indicated it was time to go. I gave the world of the living one more long, yearning glance.

Finally turning, we faced upward into a bright light. As we ascended toward it, I began to notice people on each side of me. Then I became aware: These were not just people, but people I knew and loved in life. My parents and grandparents - caresses and kisses - and old friends long gone were there, and I hugged every one. Streaming closer and closer to the light, two friends eventually came out and embraced me almost closer than my parents had. It took a second, but then I recognized, first, Tom Neil, and then,Gil. Oh, how happy I was!

He was with his family. That's all he ever wanted.

Tom and Gil now back off and signal all the others to gather around. They signal all to surround me and Barbara. Then all salute.

I don't know who said it. It seemed a much greater voice from far above and beyond.

"For the world of the living and the freedoms they will now enjoy. We thank you; you, the Revolutionist."

The End. Maybe.

Postscript

As previously stated, any resemblance between this story, its people, places and events is purely circumstantial and fictitious. Further, it is not my intention to incite riot or violence here or anywhere, but I do intend to incite controversy. That is the right of a free people, of any free people. At this writing, many situations and occurrences in my own country are very troubling. It is my personal belief that government is not adhering to constitutional law.

Our leaders have taken on monarchical powers that many citizens and even congressional members are afraid to challenge. I believe that many of our courts, police organizations and taxing authorities are either afraid to challenge supreme authority here or, more troubling, they agree with it to the detriment of our people. As a former banker, I fear that our currency is being undermined and our standard of living destroyed.

This would go along with my fear that the Environmental Protection Agency is using excessive zeal for excessive control that will destroy business and jobs in our country - our economic underpinnings - at a time when we need more businesses and jobs desperately. It is also troubling that our nation is being saturated with individuals who do not understand a free society and, as such, must be supported at great expense by our taxpayers, already heavily burdened. We all want to help the less fortunate, but impoverishing ourselves and endangering a free society will help no one in the end. This burdening taxation is forcing our educational standards to slip: unacceptable!

As one whose own grandparents spoke another language at home, I understand the problem. My grandparents and my parents taught themselves the nation's common tongue. I have traveled extensively and have seen several multi-language countries. They seldom work well, if at all. You say, "Look at

DeEarlon

Switzerland!"

I say: Thank God for the mountains that separate their different groups. A common tongue brings a common culture. A common culture brings a strong nation. That is all the more important in a large and already diverse nation. In your home, in your family, the dignity and perhaps language of your ancestors; out in the world, the common tongue, dignity and hope of your future.

Add to this that the free world is now challenged and endangered by at least three out-of-control and expanding societies that know little of, or care nothing for, freedom, and our current national leaders either ignore this or seem to actually help our adversaries. As a student of history I can tell you this is bad, very bad, and can only have one end: one that is disastrous for our people and nation.

It is an unprecedented situation our country finds itself in - and a very dangerous one. Far too many do not understand the long-term consequences of these dangers. Ignoring these clear dangers, they indulge in the overwhelming pleasures and distractions of the day: such distractions often encouraged by those in high places.

Point of fact: Those in high places are turning a blind eye to these overwhelming dangers in favor of enriching themselves in both money and power. Even if we wish to ignore these distractions, we will all personally suffer, and suffer greatly, in the long run. We stand on the precipice.

I truly hope that a situation similar to that described in this book does not develop in my country. To whit: I call on our political leaders to change course, and even more importantly, for our citizens to enlighten themselves and actually take action: politically, of course.

Without a change of course, the consequences for us all are unthinkable and may not end as happily as this story.

Thank you. Good luck and God bless to all lovers of freedom everywhere.

The Author

A true Renaissance man, DeEarlon has spent much of his life in serious academic studies of history, economics, political science and even theology. He spent over 30 years in banking and holds a degree from the American Institute of Banking. Now retired and an increasingly popular novelist, DeEarlon's studies continue today, finding expression in *The Revolutionist*, his second novel. He lives in Connecticut.

Also by DeEarlon from Barking Cat Books

Heaven's Wave: A Novel of the Doomsday Prophecy of 2012

DeEarlon

The Revolutionist

www.ingramcontent.com/pod-product-compliance
Lightning Source LLC
Chambersburg PA
CBHW070705280626
47159CB00022B/2097